A Boy

And

A War

A Boy
And
A War

S.R.Shuja

First Edition

Cover page: Moshiur Rahman and S.R.Shuja

Printed in the United States of America

Publisher: MindTalkers Publishing

ISBN #:978-0-9878187-5-1

Visit www.mindtalkers.com

To my mother Jahanara Rasheed

Chapter 1

1970.

My dad was posted in a government hospital in a town named Navaron in southern Bangladesh, then East Pakistan. He had landed this job after graduating from medical school the year before. This was a small, quiet town located near Jessore, a major city. I was five. My memory isn't very vivid about that town. My grandparent's house from father's side was in a village near the suburb called Kaligonj located in the district of Satkhira. It was only about 50 miles away from Navaron, connected by regular bus service.

Grandpa (dadu) visited us frequently bringing along grandma (dadi) and great grandma (jhima), who was his step mother and much younger than him. His dad – a rich landowner - in his old age convinced a poor family to give away their teenage daughter in marriage to take care of him. His first wife had died long ago. Little after the marriage he passed away but Jhima had stayed as a widow since. She had no children. We, her great grand children, were the jewel of her eyes. She had a great sense of humour and indulged Rushi – my kid sister - and me to no limits. In return each of us loved her to death.

Grandma (dadi) was a pretty woman who happened to be very quiet. Her display of love and affection was not very apparent but we felt it deep inside our heart. Whenever the trio visited us in Navaron we became ecstatic. Rushi was only two and had an exceptional tendency to nag just about every-thing, which often turned into incessant crying. At times this became intolerable. You coo at her she goes berserk, you cuddle with her she still goes ber-serk. My parents gave me grief believing me to be the inevitable source of all her agony. They would give a deaf ear on what I had to say. Luckily, when we had visitors she was usually better. With her tears subsided to some extent, the amount of scolding heading my way proportionately decreased.

Dad was working for East Pakistan health ser-vices. He was the assistant surgeon of the main hos-pital. Fortunately he received government housing. This was a blessing as his salary was barely enough to maintain a descent life. There was never any savings. Mom never really liked dad's job. The law and order situation in the region was deteriorating and the rate of murder was relatively high. One of dad's responsi-bilities was to issue death certificates which he ended up doing too often for comfort. Mom had been a little bit on the timid side and worried about practically everything under the sun. Even a little thing would cause a severe nervous breakdown in her.

Our house was near the hospital. Sometimes corpse bearers would pass by our house carrying the hastily covered dead bodies. If mom happened to be looking out at that moment and had a glimpse of the corpse she wouldn't be able to sleep that night. Her sleepless nights meant constant moaning and sobbing. Rushi and I used to share the same bed with our parents. On the nights when mom cried Rushi made it a routine to join mom with her signature nasal, utterly annoying crying. There was very little I could do but to listen to their wailing contest while keeping awake for most part of the night. Mom usually cried relatively quietly but not Rushi. She was loud as a horn and was incessant. Talk about nuisance! Dad was having second thoughts about his job as well. The money was nothing to brag about; in addition he had to deal with dead bodies all the time. He started to look around for other works.

In the mean time a famous circus came to Navaron. I was ready to bolt to the circus arena. I had heard so much about it! There were tigers, lions, bears, elephants! How could anybody let go such an unbelievable opportunity? I begged my dad to take me. I even bribed Rushi with some lozenges and urged her to do the same. Unfortunately she was just as scared of circus animals as mom was. The mention of tigers and bears instantly intimidated her. After constant pledging dad finally agreed to take us to the circus. We got a ride in his government vehicle.

This was my first time in a circus. The animals were simply out of the world.   Dad had hard time managing my enthusiasm. Rushi on the other hand got really scared with all the crowd and noise. She held on to mom tightly. One of the main attractions of the circus was a gigantic elephant. As we approached the elephant mom got very scared. This wasn't her first time seeing an elephant close up but it'd been a while and she seemed to have forgotten how big they actually could be. Rushi screamed in fear. Mom quickly stepped back with Rushi in her lap. I was not scared. Why would anybody fear such a gentle animal? They were also available to ride for a fee. With dad's approval I was soon placed on the back of the elephant. The animal walked in a small circle before I was brought down to the earth. I walked to mom and Rushi with a victorious smile. Mom looked nervous and pale. "How in the whole world did you ride on that animal?" She gasped.

She remained shaky even after we reached home later in the evening. She had nightmares and screamed us awake. Dad tried to be patient. How could anybody freak out just by watching an elephant?

Next morning something even worse happened. Couple of murders were committed in a distant village the night before. The dead bodies were carried to the hospital in the morning. Talk about stroke of luck – they went past right before the very eyes of my mother! She passed out immediately. Fortunately I was nearby. I ran to get the lady from our neighbouring house. She sprinkled water on mom's face and fanned her with a hand-held fan.

That night dad declared that he would actively look for other work. He had a desire to join the army for a while. It was considered to be a stable job with good salary and additional facilities. After discussing with mom he decided to give it a try. Mom was always terrified about wars. However, there was no reason to believe that a war was imminent. Pakistan was under the martial law rule of Yahya Khan. There were occasional civilian disturbances but no sign of any large scale military involvement. On the other hand dad was a physician. Even if there was a war he wouldn't be sent directly on harm's way.

Dad joined army in August, 1970 as a Lieutenant Doctor. He was posted in Comilla cantonment, East Pakistan. After one year of service with favourable reference from his senior officer he would be promoted to a Captain. Dad was very pleased. Not only he would be making more money but also would be spared from dealing with dead bodies on regular basis. This would supposedly make mom much more comfortable as well. Before reporting to his job in Comilla he left us with his parents in the village. We were to join him later once he made proper arrangement for housing. There was no housing available inside the cantonment. We didn't have to wait too long. He found a house nearby Cantonment area. Housing inside the cantonment would have been free of cost. For this one he would have to pay half the rent. With no other choice he took it and brought us there.

Comilla cantonment had a mixed population of people from both East and West Pakistan. There were several Pathans and Panjabis in dad's group. Dad's C.O. (Commanding Officer) Lieutenant Colonel Romijuddin was from East Pakistan. He was a nice person. Dad's promotion would depend on his recommendation.   The officers from West Pakistan were generally nice. Regardless, in many occasion there were disagreements between the two, primarily due to ongoing political tension between the two parts of Pakistan – East and West. Briefly, at the end of the year 1970 Yahya Khan called for an election. Sheikh Mujibur Rahman, a reputed politician from East Pakistan and the head of Awami League, won the election clearly by majority of votes from constituencies located in East Pakistan. On the other hand Zulfikar Ali Bhutto, the founder of Pakistan People's Party, won large number of seats from West Pakistani constituencies. Bhutto refused to accept an Awami League government and demanded Sheikh Mujib formed a coalition government with PPP. However, Sheikh Mujib did not agree to such undemocratic demand and as a result Yahya Khan postponed the inaugural session of the National assembly. After that the political situation started to heat up quickly. Army was no exception. More and more incidents, though minor, were observed among both soldiers and officers.

Amid this there was a talk to send dad and several other doctors to West Pakistan for training. Mom was not happy. If dad went away for training then she would have no other choice but to take her two kids and either go back to our village home to live with our grandparents or go to Khulna to stay with her older sister and her husband. Dad studied medicine after he and mom got married at an early age. Mom had to stay away from him for a while. Even after completing his degree they didn't have much opportunity to live together. The thought of living without him again put a serious strain on her. Dad tried his best to assure her that he would be taking us to West Pakistan as soon as possible. He could have taken us with him but he neither knew the country nor had any acquaintances there. He didn't feel comfortable taking the whole family with him in an unfamiliar place. However, in Karachi we had some family friend but he didn't have an opportunity to contact them. Mom went into her so familiar breakdown feat. I wasn't totally sure what she was so sad about. No matter where we went, grandparent's house or Aunt's house, it was all about running around, playing with cousins and friends, lots of freedom. Why was she so teary-eyed?

Soon we learned that the training schedule had changed. Nobody was being sent for training at that time. Was mom happy! I was slightly disappointed. Whatever! Life inside the cantonment wasn't too boring either. I made a few friends and we played all over the area. I was spared from listening to Rushi's agonizing nagging at least for some time. A few of my friends were Urdu speaking. I picked up a few Urdu words from them. Things were sort of good. The only trouble came from mom. She started to push me to study harder and harder. Did I mention she had a short temper? Most part of my evenings was spent being yelled at. It was difficult to see how somebody who got mad so easily could cry like little girls when the situation demanded.

Couple of months later dad's C.O. changed. Lieutenant Colonel Jahangir from East Pakistan became the new C.O. We heard good things about him. As time went by the differences inside the army grew steadily. It was not very apparent at first but couple of incidents over the next few months underlined it.

The first incident happened when a West Pakistani general came for a short visit. A big party was thrown in his honour where the general and his companions drank profusely. Later all officers were asked to pay an equal portion of the fat bill. Many officers who abstained from drinking refused to pay. They didn't mind sharing the price of the food but not the liquor. Dad was one of them. He was determined not to pay the Rupee 30 asked by the authorities. Some of his colleagues from East Pakistan Doctors Mohsin, Faruk, Jahangir and a few Pathans from the West heavily objected too. Most Pathans came from northern frontier of Pakistan and were much more sympathetic to East Pakistanis than the Panjabis were. Many times it was the Pathans who often sided with the East Pakistanis. After plenty of arguments and finally with the help of the high ranked officials a solution was reached. Dad and his friends wouldn't have to pay for the liquor. But the event imprinted a permanent concern in the minds of many.

The second incident took place during one of the officer's open discussion meetings. Some officers from both ends were outspoken about the current political situation. There was a fear that the existing situation could deteriorate any time. Officers from East Pakistan were clearly unhappy with the way Yahya Khan gave in to Bhutto and did not allow Mujib to form government. On the other hand officers from West Pakistan felt just the opposite. They didn't want Awami League to lead the country, regardless of the election result. They felt the politicians from West Pakistan should form the government. In the meeting dad expressed his discontent using chosen words making sure the overall tone didn't offend anybody. However, not everybody was able to keep their composure. Lieutenant Makbul from Education core became so agitated that he even went as far as to say that the state of East Pakistan had no choice but to separate. The patience had worn out and it was time for the East to throw back all the crap that West had thrown at it since the birth of Pakistan in 1947. After this the meeting turned into a screaming match between the East and West. Eventually Lieutenant Makbul was escorted out of the meeting to bring the situation under control. Later Bengali officers cordially congratulated him for speaking the inevitable, appropriate or not. The situation remained tense in the coming days.

The Bhola cyclone, a devastating tropical cyclone, struck East Pakistan and India's West Bengal on November 12, 1970. It was the deadliest tropical cyclone ever recorded with up to half a million people losing their lives primarily as a result of the storm surge that flooded much of the low-lying areas of the Ganges Delta. The cyclone practically destroyed the coastal areas of Noakhali. Villages were flattened, crops destroyed, lives lost.

Dad and his team of doctors went there to treat the sick and distressed. The devastation was so bad that they had to struggle to keep their sanity. There were bloated, rotting dead bodies floating all over the place. The survivors lived in inhuman conditions with no food or drinking water. The storm and subsequent flood had ripped open the wooden silos where the farmers traditionally stored their grains. Yesterday's rich was today's homeless. They had nothing to quench thirst, nothing to stop hunger. Dad and his team tried their best to treat the survivors. However, the supplies for food and water dripped in slowly and inadequately.

Fortunately a Hindu rich farmer with the title Sadhu (saint) opened a food kitchen in his yard. Magically his house was unharmed and he suffered very little grain loss. It was a general belief that the densely grown tall coconut trees that surrounded his house worked as a natural barrier. It must have had absorbed the thrust of the storm surge and the wind. A good and generous man Sadhu fed the hungry in his yard for two long weeks and provided shelter to the homeless. He knew that the rich farmers who had become homeless would never let go their pride to come to his food kitchen. He sent food and water to those families. Dad was impressed at his generosity. He wasn't the only farmer saved from the wrath of the calamity but none came forward with such kindness.

During one of his meeting with Sadhu when dad inquired he solemnly answered, "God saved me from this disaster. The grains that could have been destroyed by the water I am sharing that with my neighbours. This is my duty. If we can't help when others really need us then why born as a human? "

Dad never forgot about Sadhu.

Dad got selected to go for the training, once again. This time there was no talk of postponement. Mom was tense. I had to cop up with incremental berating for practically everything. Rushi seemed to nag with double intensity. Our home suddenly turned into a morbid place. I wondered what would happen when dad really left. No date for departure was fixed yet but January or February looked bright. Our friends and families were concerned. The political situation had been steadily getting worse. Going to the West at a time like that didn't seem wise. The country was becoming restless. Awami league was still not permitted to form the government.

The rebellious student body of East Pakistan was getting impatient by the day. In 1952 it was primarily the students who had initiated the Bengali Language Movement advocating the recognition of the Bengali language as an official language of Pakistan. On 21st February when police fired and killed some of the protesters a civil unrest started led by the Awami Muslim League, later renamed as only Awami league. After years of conflict the central government granted official status to Bengali language. The memory of that glorious victory was still bright into their minds. It was only a matter of time before they burst into another uprising against the West Pakistani rulers. Demand for separation hadn't been raised yet but clearly it crossed many minds. The sign of a brewing problem was evident. However, dad wasn't ready to refuse to go for training, not unless something drastic had happened. The situation in the Army was still relatively normal. Two of his friends Drs. Mohshin and Jahangir had completed their training earlier. They were both posted in Comilla.

Finally his training date was fixed in February. If we went with him government would have paid all our expenses. The same would be true if we joined him within six months. Dad did not want to take us all into an uncertain situation. We had to stay back.

There was another reason which I learned a few months later. Our plan was to stay with my paternal grandparents (dadu - dadi) for a little while and then move with mom's older sister (khala) and her family in Khulna. Dad would try his best to arrange for our trip within six months which would definitely save us a lot of money.

In January dad received a sermon from Jessore Court of law regarding a death certificate that he issued when he was working in Navaron. He was a witness for the defendants. Such sermons were normal but until then he never had to physically show up in court.   This time he had no choice. Dadu's house was only a few hours away from Jessore. He planned to take us all with him and drop us in dadu's house in the village. Once the court matter was resolved he would return to Comilla and fly to West Pakistan where his training would take place.

I was very excited. The memory of all the wonderful things in my grandparent's house flashed before my eyes – the vast fruit garden with dozens of varieties of mangos, several varieties of berries, jackfruits, coconuts, leeches etc.; the fields of sugar canes; the ponds; the cattle grazing in the fields; the magical tune from the shepherd boy's flute – all together a complete recipe for adventure. Most part of my early childhood was spent there. I rolled and crawled on the clay courtyard, toddled in the neighbourhood, grew up in the lap of the loving but dirt poor village women. Those memories got imprinted so deeply in my mind that the possibility of returning there filled me with joy and anticipation. I could barely wait.

Chapter 2

Winter wasn't totally over yet. The touch of coolness in the air felt quite good. One evening after travelling in a bus for practically the whole day we reached the tiny riverside suburb called Kaliganj. After crossing the river we would have to go another five miles to reach my grandparent's house. Dadu had already been informed about our arrival and was supposed to send a bullock cart to carry us home. One of his servants should be waiting for us with the cart on the other side of the river.

As soon as we crossed the river in a wooden rowing boat I saw the shepherd boy who took care of my grandparent's cattle. His name was Alek Mia. He couldn't have been older than fifteen. He played the pipe very well and could jump from tree to tree like a monkey. During my visits to dadu's house a major part of my time would be spent with him. Once he had secretly taken me to the grazing fields with the cattle. My disappearance had stirred up the neighbourhood with everybody searching for me. Several hours later dadi sent a domestic hand to the grazing fields – just in case. I was chasing around the calves with a stick. My safe return was celebrated with my devastated young mother relieving in stream of tears.

That evening after Alek returned from the fields and drove the cattle in the shed next to the courtyard dadu summoned him in the outhouse. Vice president of the union for many years dadu was a well known and respected person. He was a man of little words and much temper. However, I had never seen him hitting anybody. But that night he slapped Alek on the face, once, in front of everybody. He did not say even a single word. Alek was not surprised at all. He knew something of this nature was going to happen. After this incident things changed a little bit between us. We couldn't spend as much time together as before. Mom took especial effort to keep me away from him. She was a village girl but yet fostered a significant fear about the villagers. She believed that the villagers were simple minded but were also capable of committing heinous crimes. She feared that Alek might try to harm me to take revenge on dadu. That day it was I who had insisted on going with him. He really wasn't to be blamed.

Few days after that incident we moved to Navaron. Seeing Alek after a while my heart just danced on. He hugged me dearly and picked me up. I could see his eyes tearing up even in the dark. "Why did it take you guys so long?" He couldn't hide the wetness in his voice. "I was so worried."

My parents were anxious to get home as soon as possible. The overall situation of the country wasn't at its best. There was a considerable fear of being robbed on the way. Our luggage was loaded swiftly into the cart and on the road we went. One of my distant uncle lived nearby. We stopped at his place and took one of his workers to accompany us for added security. He lit a hurricane lamp and walked ahead of the cart. Time to time he yelled at the passing pedestrians and cyclists, "Who goes there?"

Inside the covered bullock cart mom and Rushi sat quietly. I sat at the back with my legs hanging out. Dad alternated between walking along with the cart and hopping on the cart to sit beside me. It was getting darker as the night encroached slowly. A crescent moon hung in the sky in the midst of the white clouds. The dirt road meandered through the paddy fields that extended to the horizon. Our cart moved slowly with a laboured sound of the wheels, joining the synchronized sounds of the fireflies to create a unique music. Every now and then isolated cyclists approached us with their bells ringing 'Cring Cring' as they leaned forward to get a glimpse of the visitors.

"Where are you heading?" The curious ones asked gently.

"Goneshpur." Alek Mia or the man with the lamp answered alternately.

"Which house?" The follow up question was inevitable.

"Habibur Morol."

"Oh!"

Not everybody recognized the man, but some did. They respectfully nodded and went in their own ways. Our cart crawled through villages after villages. We turned west after reaching Pirojpur. If we had gone south for another 3 miles we would get to my mom's parental house.

Mom had ten uncles from her father's side. Each of them had at least half a dozen children. Some of their children had grown up and started families. All together they had occupied a full village. My time there went by so quickly! The hoard of cousins ensured that I was never bored. We roamed around the village, played tag in the moonlight on the sprawling courtyard, dared the shady village roads at night to venture to the small convenience store located near the river to buy delicious treat. The freedom was incomparable, memories unforgettable. Of course, none of these would have been possible without my cousin sister Rani. She was twelve and a daredevil. Her reputation had spread far beyond her village. A merited student she was the indisputable leader of the younger kids in the village. Adults trusted her, relied on her. Even my mom stopped worrying about me when I was with her.

I shot a meaningful look toward my dad. He read my mind clearly. "Don't worry, you'll visit them," he said. "I'll tell your dadu to send you folks to Dorgahpur for a few days."

"Isn't that what he wants!" Mom chirped in. "Once there I would barely see him. He would shadow Rani everywhere."

Dad's indulgent laughter rippled in the darkness. He had grown up in the villages, roamed around the countryside with his older sister. He knew the feelings.

As we closed on to dadu's house we met a group of four men: Alek's dad Shaheed, older brother Moti and couple of young men named Liakot and Rohim, all equipped with bamboo sticks and powerful flashlights. They worked for dadu.

"Alek, is that you? Alek? Hey Alek?" Uncle Shaheed yelled. Traditionally in the villages elderly men are called uncle (chacha) and women aunt (chachi) regardless of any blood relation.

"Father!" Alek answered, relieved.

Shaheed chacha hugged dad. "Why so late? Your father has been so worried that he sent us to check."

Dad walked with him as he explained the delay due to the irregular bus service. Shaheed chacha had been a long time field hand of dadu and became an integral part of the family over the years. He had no land of his own. Dadu had allowed him to build a hut in one corner of his land close to the main house. Shaheed chacha and his family had lived there for years. He had two sons – Moti and Alek. Moti married a few years back and built another hut near his father's hut. They all had a special corner for dad. Not only he provided free medical treatment but he had also advocated for them to dadu to allow them to build a shelter in his land.

At dadu's house we were greeted by a bustling crowd who had gathered in the courtyard. Villagers in this part of the country were impoverished with a few having any kind of education. Most were field hands working for a handful of rich farmers who owned most of the farming lands. Anybody who rose above the ordinary, especially with education, were honoured and loved. When any of these successful children visited, villagers gathered to show their appreciation. Dad was special among specials and his popularity was enviable. Since becoming a licensed physician he had treated the poor villagers for free often handing over medicines free of cost as well. People came from far away, mostly the dirt poor. They took this opportunity to get a free check up, often some free medicines and a reasonably good meal, courtesy of dadi.

Upon our arrival dadi came rushing and hugged both Rushi and me tightly. Clearly she was very worried at our late arrival. That night when everybody left and we could finally get to bed it was already past midnight. In the villages most people went to bed early to save on kerosene cost. Seldom there would be exception to that. When my dad or his older brother Uncle Nowsher (chachu), a renowned teacher in the town of Satkhira, visited exceptions to that rule was made.

Dad left next morning. He had to show up in Jessore Judges court as a witness that day. Before leaving he held me lightly in his arms and said," Take care of your mother and sister. Okay?"

I nodded with pride. Why won't I be able to take such minor responsibility? Dad said goodbye to everybody and climbed up the back of a passenger bike, customarily called a *helicopter (*a regular bike with an extra seat, usually just a flat piece of rectangular wood, attached to the carrier). When only men travelled they primarily used this means of transportation. It was much faster than the bullock carts. I ran alongside the helicopter that carried dad for as long as I could. Slowly the bike rolled away out of sight on the meandering dirt road that disappeared into dense vegetation. I kept on waving until I could make out dad's silhouette against the rising sun. Tears welled up into my eyes. I wondered when I was going to see him again. He was supposed to go back to Comilla from Jessore. From there he would make the trip to West Pakistan. There was no knowing when we could finally make it there. Alek had been running with me. He quietly picked me up into his lap.

Dad had no difficulty as a witness in the court of justice. He was asked whether he had issued the death certificate, which he answered positively. The hand writing was his. After that none of the parties had too many questions for him. This was his first time in a court. He was sort of nervous. He hadn't done anything wrong but the lawyers could be tenacious at times. He felt relieved once that part was over.

He made the journey to Comilla the same day. Next morning he called Uncle Nawsher (chachu) in Satkhira to inform that he had reached Comilla safely. Satkhira was only couple of hours from dadu's house. On the following weekend chachu came down to village himself to deliver the news. Normally important news would get passed on with acquaintances regularly commuting between Satkhira and Kaligonj. On our way to the village we didn't stop by at chachu's house. An affectionate person he took this opportunity to visit us in the village. Aunt (chachi) stayed behind to take care of their house and children. They had four daughters, who were studying in school or college. They couldn't always leave house together even if they wanted to.

When chachu came to the village he took me on his bike and went around the village. He liked to meet the reputed and influential people of the village and exchanged opinions and information. He proudly introduced me as his nephew to everybody. "Rasheed's son. Greet with Salam, son."

I would sheepishly murmur a Salam, the Muslim way of greeting. When among familiar faces I could be the loudest, however in the presence of new acquaintances I became almost invisible.

One day he took me to Uncle Motaleb's house. He was dad's second cousin. He was big, well built like a wrestler. He used to work out and practiced fighting with bamboo stick. He showed some of his skills to me. He spun a long heavy bamboo stick around him with unbelievable deftness and speed as I observed with disbelief. Having no children of his own he was known for his affection for all children in the village.   He invited them in his house and told stories or showed performances with stick. Well known in the region he was considered to be an influential person.

From uncle Motaleb's house we headed toward the village market of Ratanpur.

"He is a good man but short tempered." On the way chachu conferred. "Got too many enemies. Beats up people for little things. Just the other day he pounded an insolent young man mercilessly for eve teasing. Later it came out that the young man's father is an influential person in a nearby village. The time is bad but who is going to explain that to Motaleb?"

I nodded wisely. Chachu did not discuss these matters with everybody. I knew because I shadowed him all through his visits. Not that I had any choice. He wouldn't go anywhere without me.

The village market in Ratanpur was only a mile away. Riding on the handle of chachu's bike negotiating the narrow, uneven, tree lined dirt road as we moved closer to the village market I felt an increasing presence of saliva in my mouth. On the south end of the market there were several sweet shops. One of them was Kamal's who made finger licking rasgulla (small cheese balls soaked in sugary syrup) and hot galebi (a deep fried sweet preparation). Coming to the market with chachu invariably meant getting the taste of Kamal's sweet. Apparently I had sweet teeth from very early age. Mom said when I was only a year old I screamed for molasses and wouldn't stop until got a plate full of it. Sweet maker Kamal issued a broad smile at my sight. He stirred up the hot rasgullas floating in sugar syrup in a large deep pan. "How many do you want, son? Two or four? I have fresh galebi. Just made them. Sir, should I pack a kg to take home as well?"

Chachu relaxed into a chair with me by his side. "Sure. Sure. First serve each of us two rasgullas and a pair of galebi. Pack up some for home too. His mom loves your sweet."

"When did they arrive?"

"Just a few days back. His dad has to go to West Pakistan for training. He dropped them off here. They will stay for a few months. Son, do you want some sondesh (sweetened cottage cheese)? Kamal, go ahead, give us couple of your special sondesh. He is a suck up for sweet things. Have too many stomach worms but I guess a little sweet every now and then won't do much harm."

"Sir, my sweet does not give stomach worm. This is Kamal's special sweet... I tell you sir. Ha... ha... ha... "

Rajab Ali was the owner of the solitary book store located in the market. The clothing store next to his store belonged to Naisur Rahman. Both were chachu's long time friends. Failing to do well in education they had resorted to business. Sales hadn't been great but enough to make a living. They had some paddy fields which were rented to landless farmers. In the end they did well though with considerable effort. Regardless both were very ambitious and took strong interest in politics. They would always get into loud discussions about local politics with chachu. Sometimes the national politics sipped in too. Bhutto wasn't ready to let Mujib to form government. A serious trouble seemed almost unavoidable. It wasn't quite clear what would be the impact of such events in this remote area. India was nearby, no more than two-three miles, just across the river. How would they react? How was this issue going to be resolved?

All this discussions made me sleepy. Chachu noticed. He was apologetic. "Oh, look how insensitive I am. I forgot about this little boy. What does he understand about politics? Come, Khoka. We'll go home."

We took a different route around the village to return home. Bored or not I loved to go around with him. It made me feel important. Who else would strike a serious conversation with me?

Chapter 3

Finally Dad's date of departure was fixed. He was scheduled to leave Dhaka on 7th February. I had a great desire to see off dad in the airport. But that was impossible to do when I was back in the village. Mom looked pretty sick lately and her temper had taken a leap as well. I avoided any contact with her. Who wanted to be barked at for nothing? I wondered if any airplane flew over these villages. I had serious doubt. Regardless, I didn't lose hope completely. Every morning I routinely asked dadu what date it was. Just in case dad's plane flew over us. I wouldn't have missed it for anything.

The harvesting in winter was one of my favourite events. The villages turned into a festive mode. The large courtyard of my grandparent's house would convert into an operation center. First, the grains had to be separated from the paddy. Several cows were tied by ropes around a central pole with a bearing that allowed the animals to walk around in a circle. A group of farm hands carried the harvested paddy from the fields to the yard in bundles. Another group banged these bundles on a flat wooden surface to separate the loose grains from the sheaf. Next the bundles were loosened and the sheaf of paddy spread in layers on the path of the cows who were driven to walk around and around.

The continuous movement of their hooves forced the grains to detach and pile up. The grains were collected on regular interval and new batches were placed. This was a familiar view in the villages of Bangladesh. I loved it so much that I could probably watch from dawn to dusk. The steady movement of the workers, the rhythmic shuffling noise of the cow huffs on the paddy, the brisk movement of the women preparing large pots to boil the rice and the thick sound of the wooden rice huller thudding on regular interval to remove the husk and bran from the grains – as a whole it was a memorable experience for the eyes, ears and mind. I always had this desire to team up with the farm hands and harvest the paddy from the fields with a crescent shaped knife, bundle them up and carry on my shoulder to the house. The hardship, the sweats, the dog tired labourers – it all seemed like part of an adventure. I begged my mom numerous times to let me go with Alek but in vain.

Unfortunately, this time we came too late. The harvesting had already completed. This was a great disappointment.

My grandparent's house had two separate large units with thatched roof. The main larger unit was located in the lower half of the rectangular courtyard on a six feet high mud base and faced south for good air ventilation. This unit had a bedroom where dadu and dadi slept and a cold room where rice, molasses, relishes were stored. The other unit was occupied by jhima. It was considerably smaller, had a three feet high base and faced the larger unit. Strategically put couple of mud walls created some privacy for the women behind the main house where the kitchen and a covered eating space were located. A separate back entrance allowed maid servants to go to the pond to fetch water or do other errands in the garden.

We - mom, Rushi and I - used to sleep in the same room with jhima, on a second bed. Jhima didn't do much of the household work. She was not in good terms with dadi and even insignificant things set up large scale showdowns. Dadi was not known to raise her voice but she tried her best to hold her ground against the thunderous voice of jhima. Luckily things never spilled out of control. Jhima was severely short sighted and slightly hard of hearing. She had to feel her way down the stairs to the courtyard from her terrace. I heard she had cataract. Dad planned to get her operated but didn't have time before he left. Jhima was notorious for bossing around the maids, servants and farm hands. She sat on a handcrafted mat on her terrace and called out at everything and everybody as she felt necessary. "Hey Moti, give that cow a nudge. Don't dose off." "Alek! Work faster. We don't pay you for nothing."

Nobody paid much attention to her though. She was equally liked and disliked. However, very few had the courage to take a stand against her. She had a nightmare of a tongue, especially when she got mad. She had an infinite collection of curses and marvelled in delivering them, particularly ensuring that none from immediate ancestors of the target were spared. No wonder everybody left her alone. I was the jewel of her eyes. Being the only male child in my dad's side of the family I enjoyed relatively more attention than the other kids. This was customary in villages. A male child was considered to be the one carrying the family name. Chachu had no son. My birth had brought much celebration in this courtyard, I heard. A widow and childless, jhima had embraced me with all her heart. Since birth I had always slept in her room, as a baby rested on her lap hours at a time, during sicknesses ate soup of the chickens she raised and most of all was indulged beyond belief. No matter what mischief I did, as long as I made it to her lap there was not a soul who could give me grief. Any complains were protested so vehemently that everybody just gave up. This was true about mom too, thankfully. This made my visits to grandparent's house particularly relaxing.

Life was good but not what it could be if Rani apa was there. I really started to miss her. I was hoping to make the trip to my maternal grandparents' (nana) house soon where I could pack up with Rani apa, but it just kept on delaying, for reasons that I could only blame mom for. She had been looking fairly strange lately, complaining about feeling nauseous all the time and having no appetite. It was quite evident that something mysterious was happening to her which was being kept a secret from me. Dying in curiosity finally I asked jhima, who laid it out before me with a mouth full of smile. I was going to have a new tiny brother or sister. I didn't fully understand the concept. I had no memory of the time when Rushi was born. What having a new sibling had to do with mom not feeling well was out of my grasp but I was quite disappointed because it was holding us back from going to nana's house.

One afternoon the village doctor paid us a visit. He pressed here and there on mom's belly and then declared smilingly what everybody had guessed already. She was going to have another baby. He found it surprising that it took this long to catch her pregnancy. To everybody's dismay mom looked heartbroken. She would be limited in her movements and might not be able to travel to West Pakistan to dad. She wept silently for a few days. I didn't dare to ask her anything, neither did Rushi. She kept on asking me. I said something good to comfort her. I prayed heavily for a little brother. One crying machine like Rushi was just enough for our household. Any more of that and I would have to look for foster home.

Dad's flight was on 7th February. Everybody talked about it all through the day. I anchored in the outfields with my eyes fixed on the sky, excited and restless. What if his airplane flew over us? Perhaps I could get a glimpse of it. But all my waiting went in vain. At dusk, when everybody failed, mom herself took the painful trip to the outfields and pulled me inside. "Which way did dad's plane flew mom?" I asked teary-eyed.

Mom smiled patiently. "Planes don't fly over here, son. Don't worry. We'll soon be with him."

I sighed. I wanted to go live with dad but at the same time did not want to leave my grandparent's house. And there was nana's house and Rani apa. It was a difficult choice to make.

Before going to West Pakistan my dad was promoted to Captain. The promotion became possible solely upon the good recommendation of his C.O. Colonel Jahangir who liked him very much. Not only he wrote a strong letter of recommendation, he also called dad into his office and conferred, "Once your training is complete, you'll be posted to Quetta Cantonment. Feel free to contact General Gul if you have any problem. He is Panjabi but very open minded. We are in very good terms. Don't hesitate to mention me."

Dad, along with a few others, flew for Abotabad, West Pakistan. This place was near Pindi and belonged to North Frontier Province. Dad was to receive training in the Medical Training Center located there. However, after reaching their destination they were informed that the planned training had been cancelled and they were to report to their respective work place. Dad was posted to Quetta. It was the capital of the province Baluchistan. Dad asked a day off to check around, but was denied. As a result he and few others had to start for Quetta almost immediately. Their train was to go to Lahore first and then to Quetta – one and a half day journey. They would travel from one part of the country to the other. There was no planned break in Lahore.

He met quite a few people on the train. All West Pakistani, who spoke Urdu. Dad could speak a little Urdu. He somehow managed to carry on conversations. His fare complexion and broken Urdu had many believe that he was a Pathan. This allowed some to open up their minds. It became quite clear that most were against handing over the government to Sheikh Mujibur Rahman, the undisputed leader of East Pakistan. Even though Bhutto was defeated in the election they felt he should form the government of united Pakistan. Dad quietly listened to them. There was no sense in getting into unnecessary trouble. It was clear to him that most of these people had no understanding of the concept of democracy.

Later he met an adjutant who had a different opinion. He had trained under Ziaur Rahman, a future leader of Bangladesh, in the Army center located in Kakul. This was the first time in the trip that dad met a West Pakistani who he found rational. Adjutant clearly stated, "See, I don't care about East or West. If we have set up a system where we are to elect our head of government by means of majority of votes received, then I want to stick to that. Bhutto shouldn't be coming up with all these useless excuses after he has lost in the election. If things don't get settled soon enough I fear we might get into some serious commotion. Can't say about others but I have no desire to go in a war against the Bengalis. Not only they are my compatriots, most of us also share the same religion."

Dad did not hide his true identity to him. The Adjutant must have had grown a soft corner for East Pakistan as a direct consequence of his training under Ziaur Rahman. Dad felt very homely in the company of this friendly and sensible person.

Chapter 4

Finally one day mom declared that she was feeling well enough to visit her parental house. She still had volcanic coughs and the dreaded morning sickness but not as bad as before – in her own words. Nana had already inquired several times making sure mom knew how eagerly he was awaiting her visit. Considering the drama queen she was I understood his anxiety. As for me I was counting days. I loved dadu's house the most but the totally different set of activities and attractions that waited for me in nana's house was simply irresistable. Of course, once there everything evolved around Rani apa. Having a gang of cousins enhanced the overall excitement by manifold.

Dadu arranged for our trip to Dorgahpur – nana's house. One fine morning we started on a bullock cart. The cart would return after dropping us. Nana would arrange our return trip. To spice up our slow and steady progress I resorted to my usual catch-me-if-you-can routine. I jumped out of the cart, ran ahead until I was out of breath, stood under tall palm trees that lined many parts of the dusty road and waited for the cart to catch me up. Eventually it did cover the distance with its painfully leisurely movement but I again bolted ahead and gave

it a new target. Mom and Rushi were quite comfortable under the covered hood, occasionally dosing off.

Many of our relatives lived by the road to
Dorgahpur. News travelled fast in the villages. Hearing that mom was passing by many came out of their
houses to greet her. 'Jaira! It's been so long we have
seen you..."

We had to stop. Mom remained in the cart as
the women flocked it, most with veils pulled far
down. A quick session of chit chat was inevitably followed by tears and sobs. These village women were
so emotional! Eventually we moved on, after an
eternity. Every time we were interrupted my impa-
tience grew. We were wasting time. Every stoppage
added additional one hour to our dead slow journey.
Mom read my mind and called out every now and
then, "come to me, son."

I didn't; instead I bolted ahead and picked a
tall palm tree to stand under until the cart caught me
up.

We went and went on the meandering dirt
road for several more hours crossing a number of
villages before finally approaching the rickety red
brick boundary wall of nana's house. I was instantly
pumped up. We went past by a small round man-
made lake and a Madrasa – Islamic school – built
next to it. The fading sound of a sweet voice reciting
Quran in Arabic greeted us right before Rani apa and
her army of kids broke the peace with a raucous wel-
come. Nana had married four times, under reason-

able circumstances. He had many children, most quite young. Rani apa, leading the pack, picked me up in her lap. I blushed. She must have had forgotten that I wasn't a little kid anymore.

My mom's mother died when she was only a few months old. Her older sister (khala) practically raised her. She was my mother's only sister from the same mother. Nana had two living wives (senior nani and junior nani) who lived in the same house in their separate sections. Each of them had several kids and looked beaten and weary. They came promptly to greet us. Nana was away but we were told that he would be back before nightfall. Knowing mom I was instantly alarmed. She did not disappoint me. Learning that nana decided to go out even after knowing she would be arriving today mom instantly welled up and allowed the stream of tears roll down her cheek profusely. This of course had a striking effect on the crowd that gathered around us. The sympathy that came flooding was overwhelming with senior and junior nani struggling to explain. Mom threw in some sobbing into the mixture before uttering the magic words. "Dad never loved me."

This caused a gasp in the crowd. "He'll be back soon." Senior nani carefully said. "He didn't want to go but had no choice."

"Why don't you step inside the house?" Junior nani added. "Your dad has slaughtered a goat for you."

Mom snared. "Did I come all this way to eat? Do you think I don't get goat in the city? How much did it weigh?"

"Almost 20 pounds." Junior nani cautiously replied.

"Small goat." Mom sighed. "Dad just wants me to go away."

I had never understood her very well. Why would somebody create such a big chaos about something so insignificant? Even Rushi had now started to nag. "I want to see nana. I want to see nana."

Aunt Morium, my father's older sister (fupi), who was married to mom's older brother Uncle Daud (mama), walked out in the yard briskly and took control of the situation. "Let's save the emotions for later. Jaira, come inside. Freshen up, eat something, then we'll decide what to do with your old man." She said calmly, without sounding too imposing while not leaving much room for other alternatives. "Rani, take Khoka and Rushi out to play." She spoke to Rani apa who was enjoying the circus. "Come back after half an hour. Meal will be ready. Jaira, step down carefully. Do you have any idea how many people are waiting inside the house to see you? Hold my hand."

Mom climbed down the cart. "I'll take on dad later."

Fupi nodded, "That's the right spirit."

Mama lived in a separate house next to nana's house and shared the same courtyard. Whenever we visited Dorgahpur we always stayed in mama's house. Nana had a large family and an old brick house with inadequate living space. There was no room for guests. Most meals we ate were also in fupi's house. However, occasionally senior nani and junior nani invited us to have dinner with them. Each of them had their own separate kitchen and their children usually ate with their mothers.

As soon as mom settled down I followed Rani apa in to the neighbourhood. Rushi pondered a lot before following us. I warned her, "No nagging or crying." She unwillingly agreed.

Nana had many brothers. They all lived in the same village, side by side, with each house separated by rickety brick boundary walls. We ran across the courtyards dashing through connecting rotting wooden doors, sped out into the backyard orchard where mango, berry, jackfruit, coconut trees grew in abundance, circled around the large pond and bolted into the open fields, aimlessly. Rushi was falling behind. Rani apa picked her up in the lap.

We roamed around the village constantly running into relatives who hugged, poked, patted and kissed before finally returning home in the late afternoon. We didn't have to be scared of mom. Fupi would save us. "Why did you kids come back so late?" She chided mildly. "Go on, wash up. I am serving rice. Rani, take them with you."

Mom was about to roll her eyes and say something unpleasant. Sensing it we quickly ran out of her view and headed toward the pond.

The pond had a paved dock with concrete benches and several steps that ran into the water. There were two big mango trees that leaned heavily toward the water. Both the trees bore delicious mangoes. We washed up sitting on the paved stairs and later got busy playing hopscotch on the paved platform. After about half an hour fupi personally made the trip to the dock and pulled Rani apa inside the house by the ear. We followed them quietly.

After meal we sat around the clay oven built in a corner in the courtyard. We lit dry hey to start up a small fire. Everytime we put new hey the fire leaped up triggering us to jump with our hands clapping in harmony. Slowly the last rays of the sun disappeared from the sky and the flames turned deep red and velvety as the darkness surrounded us.

Rani apa proposed to play tag. We all readily voiced our approval. In moments the quiet, shadowy courtyard turned into a noisy, screaming playground. Rushi was scared of dark to death. She hung with me grabbing my shirt tightly. We played for hours until the elders broke us up and sent inside.

Later that evening when nana finally returned home things turned quite dramatic. Mom had plenty of time to rehearse. She marvelled. First came the tears, then the sobbing followed by the deadly words that supposedly would hurt nana the most. *Nana knew she was coming today and yet didn't bother to change his plan. Why would he? If she hadn't lost her mother so early nana would never dare to neglect her all through her life.*

Nana had special soft corner for mom as she had literally grew up without the love of a mother. He chuckled foolishly. Mom went on and on until she started to feel nauseous. Nana helped her inside the house. The trouble was over for the time being. Nana had bought a nice saree for her – green body with yellow stripes and red edges. This worked magic in cheering mom up. Her sadness quickly disappeared and was replaced with cheerful giggles. It was hard to read her mind. Laughter and crying followed in random patterns.

As the night deepened our bed time was arriving quickly. Many kids had already hit the sack. Once the commotion subsided Rani apa and I left Rushi with mom and slipped out of the house. Mom had hawk eyes. She called out, "Listen! Where are you guys going?"

"Not too far. We'll be back in no time." Rani apa mumbled.

She pulled me out and we walked briskly across the courtyard, past the pond of the neighbouring house and then on to a narrow trail.

"Where are we going, Rani apa?" I asked.

"To the convenient store. Just a little ahead. They sell biscuits. You'll love it."

"What kind of biscuit?"

"They have all kinds but the one made from tamarind seed is the best."

"You can make biscuits from tamarind seed?"

"I don't know. That's what they say."

The store was a tiny shack with a flickering kerosene lamp. The store keeper was a middle aged skinny man. He smiled broadly at Rani apa. "I haven't seen you for several days, dear. Where had you been?"

"Mom wouldn't let me come after dark." Rani apa replied. "I have to come secretly. Why don't you open the store when there's still light?"

"I want to, dear, but I have a day job to attend. I can't make a living just from this tiny store. What can I get you today, my dear? Who is this boy?"

"Jaira fupi's son."

"Really? He has grown up quite a bit. When did they come? I haven't seen Jaira for long time. Son, I am your distant uncle. Tell your mother that you met Uncle Jobbar. She would remember me. As kids we played together all the time. Her mother had died early so my mom used to give her a lot of attention. Dear Rani, should I fetch some tamarind seed biscuits for you kids?"

Before Rani apa had replied a voice spoke out from the shadows. "Add in some lozenges with that, Uncle."

Rani apa didn't even look back. It was clear that she knew the man. I looked into the dark and saw a silhouette. As he stepped out of the dark his face became visible in the pale light of the lamp. He was much older than Rani apa.

"Bashir, don't bother her." Uncle Jobbar said. "Ask your parents to look for a bride for you."

"Uncle, watch your mouth." Bashir rudely replied. "Just do what I asked you to do. Give her some lozenges."

"You eat the lozenges." Rani apa strongly said. "I don't want any. Uncle, please give two taka worth of biscuits."

The man stepped foward and stood very close to her. "What's the attitude about? You don't like me?"

"She is much younger than you, Bashir." Uncle Jobbar insisted.

"Why don't you shut your mouth up?" Bashir yelled at him. "Rani, I love you. Don't worry about the age difference. I look older than my age."

Rani apa grabbed the packet of biscuits that uncle Jobbar held out and tucked in the two bank notes in his hand. She completely ignored Bashir as we started our way back.

"You can't go far. I'll find you." The voice spoke from behind.

"I am going to complain against you." Rani apa sharply said.

"Go ahead. Nothing is going to happen to me."

Rani apa started to run. I followed her. We stopped after the distance felt safe.

"Who is this man?" I asked.

"A distant cousin. Bastard! Must be twice as old as I am. Sometimes I feel like shooting him. I am going to tell dad tonight. He has been bothering me for a while now. Devil! Eat the biscuits. I'll take care of him."

Upon our return we had to face combined scolding from mom and fupi. None of them approved us venturing out after dark. Mama had returned home. He indulged Rani apa beyond limits. He saved us this time.

Next few days just flew by - roaming around the village in gangs, buying biscuits and lozenges from the village market, flying kites in the fields, arranging fake marriage ceremonies between boy and girl dolls, playing hopscotch and tag. Time passed by so quickly.

Still, there was something that I couldn't shrug off my mind. Rani apa had warned Bashir but at the end she did not tell anybody about him. I didn't like him at all and wished somebody someday would beat him up. It would be a true pleasure. If I was grown up I would have definitely stand up against that creep. I dreamt of all kind of ways to kick his ass.

One night four of us were playing a card game called Ram-Sham-Jadu-Madhu. We cut playing card shaped pieces from white sheet of papers and wrote the words Ram, Sham, Jadu and Madhu on them, four of each. The cards were then distributed among four players. Game continued until somebody had all four of the same cards in hand. We played as a hurricane glowed dimly providing just enough light for the eyes to work. Suddenly our little card game was interrupted by a familiar voice. It was Alek. Surprised I heard mom inquiring, "What are you doing here, Alek? Is everything alright?"

Alec mumbled something back which I couldn't make out. Curious I stepped out. Alek hugged me.

"How are you, bud? Are you having lots of fun?"

"What's wrong Alek bhai?"

Alek smiled displaying the full set off long, uneven teeth. "Your chacha, chachi and Minu apa came. They want to see you. They sent me to take you all home."

For a split second I felt disappointed. Minu apa was a bit older than me but she loved me very much too. My time with her was something to cherish for as well.

"Did you bring the cart, Alek?" Fupi asked.

"Yes. It's on the front yard. We have to start early tomorrow. It gets pretty hot later in the day."

Mom didn't look very happy. "Can't even stay a few days in peace." She muttered in despise. "Who asked them to come now? Damn!"

"Can I go too, mom?" Rani apa begged fupi. "My school will be closed for next couple of days."

"How will you come back?" Fupi asked, not fully blowing away the idea.

"Why, Alek could bring me back on the back of his bike. Hey Alek, do you have the extra passenger seat attached to your bike?"

"Of course!" Alek replied with a grin. "I sometimes use it as a helicopter. I could drop her off. Don't worry about it at all."

Fupi furrowed her brows. "Ask your father. He might get mad at me later."

It took some clever pledging but finally Mama gave in to Rani apa. We were overwhelmed in joy. The night passed by in a blink. Next morning we woke up before dawn and boarded the bullock cart. It struggled its way through the first light of the day on the familiar dirt roads. On the way, Rani apa and I took every opportunity to jump down the cart, ran far ahead and waited for the cart to catch us up. Five miles just flew by.

Chachu greeted us cheerfully. "Finally you guys are here. Is that Rani? Good to see you dear. Minu! Did you see who are here?"

Minu Apa came rushing. "I have been waiting so long!"

It didn't take us too long to gather up some of our distant cousins who lived next door to form a gang. A picnic was planned with overwhelming enthusiasm. Minu apa and Rani apa were the natural choices for cooks. Rest of us collected dried sticks and leaves for the fire. A make shift oven was built by digging a small hole in the ground and making room for air to pass. One of dadi's chicken was slaughtered and cooked with home grown potatoes and plenty of spices. It smelt so good that we could barely wait to gorge on it. Even some of the adults came to check what was cooking Rice was boiled. Alek and I went to the banana groves and cut a bunch of long leaves, which we cleaned and divided into smaller dinner plate size pieces. Later we sat in a circle and ate on the banana leaves. Mom, chachu and chachi also joined us for the meal. Incidentally, the chicken curry had no trace of salt in it but that didn't stop us from savouring it. "Damn! I forgot to put any salt in it." Rani apa admitted bitterly.

We broke into laughter. One of the maids brought some salt which was passed along the circle. All was fine.

Rani Apa returned home after couple of days. Mama missed her so much that he personally came to take her home. I was a little sad as mama paddled away with Rani Apa in his bike.

"Don't be sad." Mom said. "We'll visit them again. Soon."

Hope was all I needed to feel better. I packed up with Minu apa and explored the neighbourhood visiting some of her friends in between. Generally the villagers had admiration for the Morol family – dadu had been the vice president of the Union for many years, chachu was a reputed teacher in Satkhira and dad was a passionate physician who volunteered his service to the poor. People patted on my back and said encouraging words, mostly demanding that I followed the trend of the family, especially because I was the oldest grandson, at that point the only one. This was somewhat indulging but mostly stressful. Who ever wanted to bear such high expectation on such small shoulders?

Lately we were having grandiose meals in rural standard. Dadi slaughtered a chicken or a duck almost every day. Dadu bought beef or goat meat from the village market. Chachu and chachi ate very little but dadi wouldn't listen. I didn't have to be a genius to figure out dadi had a special bonding with chachu, her first child. Perhaps my mom and I had the same. I just wished it didn't get so personal at times in the form of screaming, berating, yelling and all other things closely related.

Visitors came in regular interval, mostly the village elders. They sat in the outhouse in flickering hurricane light and engaged into loud discussions, almost always about politics. Yahya Khan didn't accept Sheikh Mujibur Rahman's six point demands, the first and foremost being - the constitution provided a Federation of Pakistan in its true sense on the Lahore Resolution and the parliamentary form of government with supremacy of a legislature directly elected on the basis of universal adult franchise was allowed to be established on the basis of electoral majority. Public support in East Pakistan was gaining rapidly. People of East Pakistan had given their verdict. The leaders of West Pakistan were using the smoke of nationalism to suck up the juice of East Pakistan. They cared nothing about the welfare of the people of this country. Why would anybody trust them? Mujib was right. We needed self-governing rights. Our own kind will be our leaders, not someone from West Pakistan.

The discussions continued deeper into the night. Trying hard not to dose off all I could make out was that Yahya and Bhutto were the villains and Mujib was our hero. One day Mujib was going to beat the hell out of them. I neither tried nor understood anything more than that. The problem was chachu wasn't getting the message. Alek used to sleep at one corner of the outhouse, in a small room. He would cough quietly when he wanted to attract my attention. I would then mumble ineligibly about peeing or getting a drink and slip out. Two of us would then make our way through the vegetable garden to the rear pond and sit by the water. A bamboo flute would appear magically in his hands. He could play the tragic tunes with such passion! It was so appealing that even the ghostly creatures who resided in the nearby dense bamboo groves stopped to listen to the tune. At least that's what some people believed. The thought of such ghoulish existence brought shivers in my body.

The village elders organized a meeting before chachu left. The overall situation of the country was turning bad and a general unrest was not out of question. How would the villagers handle such situation? What would happen if God forbidden a war broke out? The meeting took place on the courtyard of dadu's house. Wobbly chairs and hand crafted carpets were offered to the attendees based on social distinction. The commoners stood in a semi circle at the end of the gathering. The courtyard was crowded to maximum capacity. Uncle Motaleb, a diehard supporter of Mujib, attended and addressed the crowd with his usual bluntness. He demanded that if a war broke out all adults must sign up. Young men in the village seemed to get quite excited at the possibility of war. Alek's older brother Moti Bhai voiced his unconditional devotion to Mujib. War or unrest – he wasn't going to miss any. Shahid chacha's face darkened. He looked worried and dejected but laboured to look brave. This definitely wasn't the time to display fear.

As the chief speaker chachu spoke calmly. Yes, the possibility of war was real but a peaceful resolution was most desirable. Yahya khan couldn't have been a total idiot. How could he not see that a war against East Pakistan would be devastating for both East and West? War was not in the best interest of anybody.

While the adults continued with their speeches, discussions and occasional arguments, the kids took it one notch up. We ventured in the fruit orchard at the back of the house and started a battle. The dry fallen branches became our guns, our screaming mouths did the rest as we tried to shoot each other down ...bang...bang...whoosh...whoosh...POW...POW...We continued into the dusk totally oblivious about the proceedings of the meeting.

It was almost dark when the meeting finally ended. People returned to their homes in small groups. I heard pieces of discussions, some for the war, some against. Some wanted independence; some wanted to stay integrated as Muslim Pakistan. They did not want to pack with India. The despicable Hindus! The disrespect and distrust was crystal clear. I had already started to fall into the dubious effect of religion by then. There was no doubt in my mind that the Muslims were much better than the Hindus, though I wasn't quite sure about the reasoning be-hind such belief. The few families of Hindus who lived in our village were all poor, hard working people. There was no lack of nicety in their behaviour. Hindu men wore dhuti, a long piece of cloth, as oppose to lungi, a sewn piece of cloth that Muslim men wore. Hindu married women put vermillion or Sindoor at the parting of the hair and maiden girls put dots on their forehead, often matching the color with their dress. I had noticed some Muslim women using dots as well. I heard that the Hindus ate turtles, crabs and pork. I never saw them eating but they were sold in the village market. Komol da, who worked for dadu, processed the date trees to collect sap in the winter and carried the round belly clay containers full with sweet sap in the mornings to my grandparent's house. That sap was then boiled in large containers over clay ovens to make dense molasses. Just the other day he had smilingly called out, "How are you little brother? Why didn't you come during the sap time? Did you eat the molasses? The molasses that your grand ma makes has a special taste to it."

Komol da was a good person. He had a large swell on his forehead. Dad said it was a tumour. One time I visited their house and had some sweets that they distributed after worships, which brought me some scolding from mom. Alek got even more for taking me there. However I had visited the houses of many Hindu families with chachu and even ate the meals they offered. Chachu never considered them different than us.

Chachu and his family left after a few days. Dadu looked very worried. Mom wanted to visit nana again but he (dadu) wouldn't allow. The political situation was not good. Our village was very close to the Indian border. He felt it was probably a better idea for us not to stay in the villages at all. Mom became nervous and started quite a tantrum. "Didn't I tell him not to go to West Pakistan for training? He left us here in this village all by ourselves. What are we going to do if the war starts?" She lamented.

Jhima couldn't contain her annoyance. "Can you stop blaming our son for a moment?" She barked.

Mom paid no attention to her. I only prayed she didn't lose her cool. I had seen them going at each other. It always turned into a screaming match and wasn't a pleasant experience for the hearing mechanism.

After much pondering it was decided that we'll move to Khulna and stay with khala until dad returned or we made the trip to wherever he was. The thought of leaving the village made me sad but at the same time I was elated with the thought that life in Khulna wasn't too boring either. With khala and khalu over indulging, a pair of older cousin brothers – charming and constantly bickering, a hilariously interesting young domestic help – there was not much room to complain. It never felt anything but a second home.

Chapter 5

Decided but we still had to hold off the trip to Khulna until mom felt well enough to make the trip. Her pregnancy seemed to have frequent ups and downs – screaming at me one moment, all nauseous the next followed by nasty throw ups. Even going to Dorgahpur could be a struggle. Dadu knew he had no other choice but to take us in person to Khulna. Mom, in her current condition, could never handle an escape artist and a crying machine. However, he was in the middle of a land dispute and couldn't leave right away.

My life went on uninterrupted. In every opportunity I got I wandered away into the village. This was particularly a concern to mom. She never missed an opportunity to lecture me on the dangers of such ventures. Only if I could grasp the gravity of it! My time was spent doing the usual – roaming around in the orchards, listening to Alek's tune on the pipe, shepherding the cattle in the grazing fields, fishing in the pond with a hook on a fixed line tied at one end of a dried jute stick and so much more. Time breezed through.

Once she was feeling a little better mom demanded to revisit his parental home one last time before going to Khulna. This was good news. I was drooling to join Rani apa again and ploughing through the neighbourhood. Alek was asked to take necessary preparation which really meant he had to find somebody to take the cattle out for grazing. Unfortunately, the date kept on getting pushed back. Thanks to mom who never seemed to feel better for long enough to make the trip safely. She was nauseous and miserable all the time. Some days she barely got up from bed. Who knew carrying a baby was so much trouble!

One day I was riding with Alek on his bike to the village market when we crossed the postman, who stopped us.

"Hold on Alek. Isn't he Rasheed's son?"

"Yes, the only one." Alek answered. Then to me, "Khoka, this is Ahmed bhai. He is our postman." Back to postman. "Do you have anything for us?"

"Do I?" Ahmed bhai graciously said. "I was actually going to their house. I have a letter from Rasheed. Do you want it, son?"

I jumped down from Alec's bike. "Yes, yes."

The postman held out a colourful envelop at me. I was delighted with the picturesque stamps. I snatched it from his hand and bolted toward home. Alek followed me in his bike.

"Jump up on the bike, Khoka. How long are you going to run?" He called out.

True. I rode on the handle of his bike as he flew through the uneven dirt road. We could hear Ahmed bhai laughing happily behind us.

The letter created a ripple of emotions in the house. After travelling through several hands it finally reached dadu. It was addressed to him. He tore off one side of it carefully and pulled out two neatly scribbled pages. The rest of us sat on the floor in a semi circle as he proceeded to read it loudly.

Dad was posted in Quetta. His training was cancelled. There was no time for that. Situation could turn bad abruptly. Preparations for war were in place. Dad did not get any housing there. He was staying in the officer's club for the time being. He didn't know how long he would stay in Quetta. There was already word of posting him somewhere else, which could be even further. He missed all of us very much. He was trying hard to take us to him but everything depended on him finding some kind of damn housing. Everything seemed to be heading for turmoil. His working environment was yet to be impacted by politics but one could easily see subtle signs. The soldiers had differences in opinions which came out during several incidents. Like several other Bengali doctors dad kept quiet. There was no good in getting into unnecessary trouble. If the situation really turned into a full fledge confrontation then the time would come to decide. He was determined not to work for the West Pakistani army. However, there was no reason to believe that they would release him so easily. He wrote many other things. At one point dadu stopped reading and passed on the letter to mom.

"The rest is for you, dear."

Mom was all tears. She took the letter and locked herself in a room. Clearly she wasn't having much of a good time without dad around. Rushi, with tears rolling down non-stop from both her eyes and nostrils, banged on the closed doors. I took her away from there and followed Alek to the cow shed. Jhima had two cows. One of them was quite pregnant just like mom. As we allowed Rushi to feel her bloated belly she became quiet. The pregnant cow watched her with big, affectionate eyes. Rushi thoughtfully said, "Is she going to have a girl like me?"

At this both Alek and I burst into laughter. "Yes she will. You'll see." Rushi adamantly said. "She is not going to have a brat like you. Neither will mom."

Not good. "Don't say such inauspicious thing." I gravely said.

That day we didn't even see mom again until it was supper time. Finally when she decided to step out of her room her face was swollen like a water-melon. It was clear that she cried to her heart's content. Jhima screamed at her mercilessly for breaking down like that. She was concerned about the baby. That night it was decided that we would go to nana's house for a second visit in couple of days. Once we returned from there we would be heading for Khulna. Dad specifically instructed mom in his letter to go to Khulna and stay with khala. He didn't think it would be safe to live so close to the border area.

Chapter 6

During my next visit to nana's house I had the opportunity to experience two unique things. One was exorcism and the other one was sanctified stick manoeuvre.

I had heard a lot of stories from Rani apa about Jinn (Genies) and Pari (Fairies). In the villages people had strong beliefs in those. What I learned from Rani apa was that Jinn - the male form and Pari - the female form were made of fire. The Qur'an, Islam's religious text, stated about these life forms. They were invisible during daytime. Among them there were good types and evil types. It was the evil ones that gave much trouble to men. Most villagers claimed to have some kind of encounters with Jinn and Pari. The general consensus was that while they were unable to harm the strong minded people they frequently took over the mentally weak. Once taking over, they were able to force that person to do things according to their wishes. It was quite common in the villages, confirmed Rani apa. She even told a few supporting stories that gave me goose bumps. One time a Jinn pretending to be a human pushed one of our distant cousin brother into the river. Our cousin brother knew how to swim and was able to save himself. In another incident a Pari had forced a young man to climb up a tall palm tree where she kept him imprisoned for three long days. Later when an exorcist was called and he performed some routines the Pari ran away. The young man climbed down the tree and asked in bewilderment, "What's going on? What are you all doing here?"

Most villagers believed the bamboo grove was the primary housing for the Jinn and Pari-s. Walking through bamboo groves at night was very risky. There was no way to know if an evil Jinn was waiting to possess you.

Anyway, the whole village knew my junior nani was possessed by one of the Jinns. Normally, she was a jolly, happy person. However, when the Jinn possessed her she would become a completely different person. The events about her encounters with Jinns had spawned many stories, some hair rising. Even the kids knew most of them. They were remembered in chronological order – by year and season. An example would be 'Summer of 1967'.

Despite having heard tons of stories that were more than enough to make me lose several nights' sleep I was yet to experience an event where Jinn and Pari-s were directly involved. This time around I got lucky. On the afternoon of the day we arrived, junior nani suddenly collapsed on the ground right in front of the house, no warning given whatsoever. Her eyes rolled up, teeth tethered. We were playing in the courtyard. Within seconds the customary leisurely scene of a village family at the approach of dusk broke into pieces and was replaced by pure chaos. "Junior nani repossessed." Somebody screamed. "Jinn! Jinn! Come quick." People ran in from all corner of the village. It was perplexing how quickly news travelled there.

By the time Rani apa and I managed to push through the crowd and got close to junior nani somebody had moved her from the door step and laid her on a handmade carpet on the porch. Junior nani was awake and looked around her - baffled, as if she didn't recognize anybody. She had this weird, possessed look. Most who gathered around her looked calm, being quite familiar with this situation. Some asked bizarre questions.

"What's your name?"

"Where do you live?"

"What's the current time of Saudi Arab?"

"How many of you are here?" Etc.

The spooky part was that junior nani answered them promptly, her voice turned heavy, rough, manly, nothing like her normal high pitch tone. The Jinn's name was Islon. He was the only one who possessed junior nani. He lived nearby, in one of the bamboo groves. Of course! He wouldn't elaborate on which one. The question answer session continued for more than ten minutes. I stood there with my eyes popping out, gulping every bit of the words that were told and heard, while holding Rani apa tightly in one hand.

"Don't be scared." She whispered in my ears. "Jinns cannot harm the little kids. We carry angels with us. They are our friends. Bad Jinns cannot enter where the angels are present."

I swallowed visibly. I had heard the same about the angels. I just hoped they didn't take an untimely break leaving me all alone to fend off these ghostly presences.

Finally an exorcist – 'ojha' in village term, rushed in and stood right next to junior nani. "Get out before I get really mad." He barked meanly at the top his voice.

"Can I stay a little longer, please?" The Jinn muttered.

"Not even a second." Ojha warned. "Get out! Are you still here? Hold on. I am going to beat the crap out of you."

He reached out into his bag and pulled out a thin stick. "Rani Apa, is he going to beat junior nani?" I asked, baffled.

"Not junior nani, actually the Jinn." Rani apa whispered. "Until he leaves all the strike that falls on junior nani's body will actually hurt him."

It was a difficult concept to apprehend. The audience however looked pumped up for the ensuing beating. Fortunately the Jinn left before the beating started. Junior nani suddenly shook his body and sat up erectly. "What's going on here? What are you all doing here?"

Ojha smiled. "That bad Jinn had taken over you once again, sister. The moment he saw me, he just ran away with his life in his hand. Ha...ha...ha..."

Junior nani quickly pulled her cloths around her body and disappeared inside the house. Disappointed, the crowd disbursed quickly. Nobody thought the Jinn would give up without a fight. It was a big letdown. People had come from far corner of the village leaving their household works. Bad, lazy Jinn! Rani apa pulled me out into the orchard in the backyard.

"Thanks God, it resolved quickly. I don't like what this ojha does. A few years back a farmer's daughter got possessed by a bad Jinn. This creep must have had done something wrong because the girl died. I don't think he knows what he is doing. I told my mother, if I ever get possessed she must not call this ojha for treatment."

My whole body shivered, a cold feeling ran down the spine. "Are you going to be possessed?"

Rani apa burst into laughter. "No way! Don't be so scared. I just wanted to be on the safe side. Let's go to uncle Jobbar's store."

Wonderful proposal! I was all ready to bolt. However, Rani apa abruptly changed her mind. "Forget it. That bastard is anchored there all the time, along with his friends. Let's send the shepherd boy."

I understood her problem. We sent the shepherd boy to get us two taka worth of tamarind seed biscuits and sat on the grass by the pond and threw rocks and dried clay in the water. In the peaceful surrounding of the ensuing evening the ripples that propagated through the calm water looked very pleasing to the eyes.

"I heard you guys are going to Khulna." Rani apa sounded a little unmindful.

"Yes, dad wrote it is not safe in the villages."

"He is right. People have changed. If a war really breaks down then we'll probably head for Khulna as well. I heard dad and mom discussing about it."

"Is there really going to be a war? Against who? India?"

"Nope. Pakistan vs. Pakistan. We are East Pakistan and they are West Pakistan. They don't want our welfare. That's why our people are mad. I hope there's no war. War kills people, wastes girls."

"How does it waste girls?"

"You won't understand. There are lot of evil people in this world. During a war not only the enemy, even friends take the opportunity. If the war breaks out I'll definitely go to Khulna. When is uncle planning to take you guys in West Pakistan?"

"Don't know. Dad wrote that he is trying. But he can't find a place for us to live."

"Don't worry. He'll find a place very soon. Do you miss him?"

"Sometimes."

The shepherd boy returned with the biscuits. All three of us sat by the pond and devoured his purchase.

Next morning I had barely waken up when Rani apa pulled me out of the house. "Totally forgot." She said excitedly. "Today there will be sanctified stick manoeuvring in uncle Naser's house. Hurry up. We don't want to be late."

I was surprised. "What is sanctified stick manoeuvring?"

"You'll see in no time."

I followed her silently. We took the backdoor, hurried through the fruit orchard, climbed over neighbours boundary fence, ran past a narrow trail through a bamboo grove, and finally stepped into the walled courtyard of uncle Naser's house. Rani apa was right. The place was jam packed with curious onlookers. They stood in a large half circle with a middle aged man standing at the center. The man held a polished piece of thick bamboo stick, seven feet or so in length. He spun the stick in lightening speed over his head in regular interval and viciously cried out , "Go get the bugger! Go get the bugger!"

In one end of the courtyard sat uncle Naser on his high back mahogany chair, his brows furrowed, face grave. Clearly he wasn't in his best mood. Near him stood three young men – pale as corpse. The middle aged man, who was being referred to as a wizard, looked directly in their direction. A little later, putting together little snippets of information that she could gather from the audience, Rani apa briefly explained the situation to me. Uncle Naser's golden watch had been stolen. It disappeared right from his room. At stake was honour and not necessarily money. Two days had passed and the watch was still missing, even after he had offered a reward. He suspected one of these three young men had stolen it. They worked in his house as day labourers. His repetitive appeal to them to return the object fell in deaf ears. Finally he asked for the help of Pagla Kanai, the wizard with the sanctified stick. Pagla Kanai looked alert, probably too much, could be the result of some cheap drug in his system. His face was hard and mean; eyes sharp and bulging.

Kanai Pagla gave a sudden scream accompanied by another display of his spinning skill before stopping to pick two healthy young men of his choice from the crowd to assist him in the process. In his instruction the two men grabbed the other end of the stick. A short meditation seemed to send him off to a mystical state as he pulled the stick with monstrous force as the two young men tried in vain to stop his advancement. The stick looked alive in his hand as he pushed his way toward the three sweating day labourers, inch by inch. It menacingly moved back and forth as Kanai screamed fearsomely, "Go get the bugger! Go get the bugger! Give the golden watch back or I'll eat the head of your mother."

And to the amazement of the crowd one of the labourers bolted out of the group and fell on the feet of Uncle Naser. His words became gibberish as he broke into a heartbreaking wail. The audience burst into a loud applause. Pagla Kanai spun his stick in lightening speed over his head one last time as acknowledgement. Uncle Naser slapped the thief several times on the face. "Where's my watch? What did you do with it?"

"I sold it, chacha. My son has eye problem. He needs to be treated. I had no money to take him to a doctor. I beg for your forgiveness, chacha."

"No forgiveness for you." Uncle Naser yelled. "My father gave me that watch. Who did you sale it to?"

Another smack on the face and the thief gave up the name. Rani apa pulled me out of there.

"Why did he steal?" I asked, looking for more details.

Rani apa sighed. "During harvest time a rice grain had hit his four year old son in the eye. That eye is about to go bad. If he doesn't get treatment he'll lose that eye. I know the man. His name is Aman Ali. He is a good man. Poverty can make people do bad things. There's too much poverty in the villages."

We suddenly found ourselves face to face with a healthy young man. I could not recognize him but looking at Rani apa's grave face I assumed this man was Bashir. He gave a wide smile. "Why do you turn so grave at my sight, Rani? I am not a bad person. Do you know how much property I have?"

"Your dad's, not yours." Rani apa bitterly said. "But I don't care about property. You are much older than I am. Please don't keep bugging me."

Bashir smiled with all his teeth exposed. "Age is nothing. Love is all. I am crazy for your beauty."

Rani Apa gave a quick jerk in my hand and ran away from there. I followed her closely. We could hear Bashir breaking into a loud laughter. A few of his friends joined him too. Rani apa didn't stop until we reached the orchard at the rear of nana's house. Both of us gasped for air.

"Bastards like Bashir don't let the girls get a good education." Rani apa muttered, once she caught her breath. "Parents have little choice but to get their daughters married early. Their life ends before it starts. I'll definitely move to Khulna."

I was ecstatic. "That would be great! We'll have so much fun. You could stay with us in khala's house."

"Let's see what dad says." Rani apa thoughtfully said. "Do you want to throw rocks in the pond? Let's go."

The pond sent away waves after waves as we kept on throwing rocks into it. We spent hours doing so, quietly.

Chapter 7

We started from nana's house at dawn. Rani apa walked as far as a mile along with the bullock cart. It was clear she didn't want to stay in the village anymore. She walked up to the village market of Tetulia before stopping. She waved as far as I could see her. Mom said, "She is very loving."

I was sad. I wish I could take her with us. She needed to be moved from here for her best interest. But who was going to pay any attention to a kid's opinion.

A few days later we started for Khulna with dadu. Alek dropped us to the boat ramp of Kaligonj. We crossed the river on a paddle boat to catch the bus that took us to Satkhira. We stayed overnight in chacu's house. The house was within the city limits but wasn't very urbanized. The two storied building had a large orchard in the rear with trees like mangos, berries, jackfruits. Minu apa had planted beautiful flowers at the front of the house. The garden had many blooms of roses. Rushi liked roses. Minu apa picked some for her. She was ear to ear smile.

"Situation is turning bad, exactly what we suspected." During supper time chachu gravely said. "National assembly has been postponed for indefinite period. Movement of Pakistani soldiers has increased. Yahya khan and Bhutto are up to something. I have a bad feeling. "

"I heard he made Tikka Khan the military governor of East Pakistan." Dadu said. "Who is going to submit to that?"

Chachi rarely participated in these discussions but today even she could not keep quiet. "God is sure to punish them. He is never going to tolerate this quietly. I fear for all these Hindu families who have been living in the vicinity of my house for decades. Poor, hard working people. If war breaks down, what will happen to them?"

Chachu smiled. "Worry about them later, dear. Fear about your own family first. What makes you think that they would spare you just because you are a Muslim? War is devil's weaponry, it spares none."

After supper two other teachers who taught in the local college stopped by. They engaged into long discussions with uncle and dadu. At night I found mom sobbing. I knew she was scared. With dad away she had no one to lean on. I wanted to soothe her but didn't brave it considering how peevish she was lately. I quietly prayed. Allah, let everything be good again. The faith on celestial matters at that age was incomparable.

We climbed into a bus the very next day, destination Khulna. Mom was very uncomfortable moving around with her big belly but what other choice did we have? Once we settled into khala's house in Khulna mom clearly wasn't planning another trip soon. She declared that in every opportunity she got.

We reached Khulna at dusk. We climbed up into two of the waiting rickshaws and asked to be taken to lawyer Mosabber's house. The rickshaw pullers stormed through the light traffic and dropped us in front of the wide iron gate of khala's two storied house on the street named cemetery road. This was a very familiar gate. Rushi and I jumped down the rickshaw and ran inside the house. Khala and khalu already knew we were coming. They hugged us dearly. "Where is your mom?"

Mom seemed to lose all her strength at the sight of her sister and brother-in-law. She had to be carried inside the house. Khala had set up a room for us to stay. Mom was taken in that room where she collapsed on the bed. She embraced khala and burst into tears for apparently no reason. Soon Rushi glued herself to mom and joined her in the wailing as well. I shrugged in despair and went on to the top floor to look for my cousin brothers, Moni bhai and Roni bhai. Usually in the evenings they gathered in the roof top den with their friends. In their late teens both were healthy, worked out with weights and had reputation as gangsters, a term used loosely to describe young men with attitude. They received plenty of respect from the local boys. Most times they would play cards in their den. Usually carefree and happy they went along considerably well but there were times when fight would break down between them owing to differences triggered by various issues - from wearing a shirt without prior approval to hitting on the same girl. The fights invariably brought commotion in the neighbourhood as both had a fascination for swearing, something they marvelled in, and opted for more howling and banging than just getting outright physical.

I walked across the flat roof to reach the den at the other end. The den was structurally complete but had no electricity. They played under the light of hurricane. The shadowy roof reminded me of the villages after dusk. I fearfully checked around. Khala's house bordered a Christian cemetery. Who knew why such a cemetery was created in the middle of the town? It was a well known fact that ghostly presences inhibited the place. I had seen them in my own eyes. One time I slept on the open roof along with Roni bhai and Moni bhai. At midnight I woke up for a totally unknown reason and noticed strange lights running around right over my head. I remained motionless for the rest of the night. I heard the best way to deter those ghostly creatures was to act dead. They might have looked like pulsing crickets but in reality were monsters in disguise, I already knew. That was the last time I slept on an open roof.

Next to the cemetery there was a muddy pond, the kingdom of the mosquitoes. Around this pond were several thatched huts where few Hindu families made their homes. They were clearly poor, lived in village like settings with hurricane as their only source of stable light.

I stood halfway down the roof and called out, "Moni bhai! Roni bhai!"

After several tries I got their attention. The door opened and both the faces peeked into the darkness. "When did you guys arrive? Why are you standing there? Hop in here."

I briskly walked into their den. It was filled with smoke. I detected a few beer cans as well. Moni bhai blinked at me. "Don't say it to anybody. It's okay for the grownups to try it sometimes. Not for you though. You may get drunk and make a big show. Ha...ha...ha..."

Everybody broke into laughter.

Roni bhai pulled me close to him. "Don't listen to him. Drunken bastard! Sit beside me. I am getting all the bad hands. How is khala?"

"Anytime now. Her belly looks like a big balloon."

This caused another burst of laughter. "You shouldn't talk like that, idiot." Roni bhai said. "Pick up my cards. Let me see how lucky you are."

Looking at the bets I figured out they were playing flash. Moni bhai was winning. Everybody else was losing including Roni bhai. My presence did not change his luck much.

After supper as mom and khala sat in the attached grilled veranda along with a few neighbouring women for a chat, in the absence of anything better to do I stationed myself nearby and kept my ears open just in case something interesting came up. Rushi had gone to sleep long ago. Moni bhai was out. Roni bhai was having a smoke on the front yard. Both of them had to smoke right after any meal, religiously. Khalu did not come for supper today. He was a lawyer and seemed to be extremely busy most of the time though rarely missed supper – the only time when all members of the house ate together. He was also a leader of Muslim League and frequently hosted party meetings in his chamber. That day he was having a meeting with the local leaders of his party. We heard noisy arguments in regular intervals coming from his closed chamber. Every now and then his voice rose over others. "Sheikh Mujib wants to sell this country to India. He wants us to become slaves of the Hindus. Muslims must remain together. If there are any issues we must resolve that politically. We are not going to hold hands with the agents of India. What do you guys think?"

The audience howled in support. Encouraged, khalu spoke with even more enthusiasm. Khala looked worried. "I really fear for him." She told mom. "Now it's time of Awami league. They have supporters all over the country. People want freedom. These religious themed ideas don't work anymore. "

"Why doesn't he change party?" Mom said. "Everybody does. Just go with the wind."

"Not him!" Khala bitterly said. "He is about sincerity and honesty. He is never going to switch."

I was tired and fell asleep soon.

The main two attractions of khala's house were their long time servant Yunus and a pet parrot. The parrot was very fond of Yunus. He had taught it to say several words. Yunus was probably fifteen or sixteen year old. Some of his favourite things were to blow big bubbles with his saliva through his lips and to make inappropriate remarks at the other young female servants who worked in the neighbourhood. He had worked really hard to teach the parrot phrases like the following: "Get out! Get out!"; "Hello beauty!"; "Mr. Lawyer steals money" and many others of same quality. When somebody stood before its cage the parrot would randomly say something at that person. One time after it called khalu "Hello beauty!" he got so mad that he took off his sleepers and beat Yunus until both the straps snapped. He then threw the pair at him and asked him to go to the cobbler and get them sewed.

Yunus was away for a few days visiting his family in the village. Once he returned my boredom evaporated completely. We started to venture out in the town. Even though he was a domestic help he rarely did any work in the house. Khala was very annoyed with him, naturally. But she couldn't drive him away either. Yunus's father had left him in this house when he was just a little boy. Yunus had become almost like a child. He did get smacked by khalu every now and then but so did Moni bhai and Roni bhai on regular basis as well. That was part of life, Yunus reasoned. One day he even took me to a movie theatre to watch the matinee show. After returning home I proudly disclosed it to mom and Rushi. The outcome was not very pleasant. Khala gave him a good smack on the back with a roller used to make flat bread. "How could you take a little boy in a movie theatre? Don't you have any common sense?"

Yunus avenged that by blowing several bubbles with his saliva at her back. With his close guidance I quickly progressed to marvel in the art of blowing bubbles with saliva. When Rushi reported this to mom I had to suffer severe humiliation in her hand. I learned that it was not a good practice. When I questioned how come Yunus could do it and not me she lowered her voice and gave me an earful. "Don't compare yourself with him. He is a servant. Your father is a doctor. How can you act the way he acts?"

I didn't fully grasp it but made mental note to be aware of Rushi. The older she was getting the more trouble she was turning out to be. Girls were always trouble, I concluded.

One morning I had just finished my breakfast with khala's handmade flat bread and a piece of white sweet ball (rasgolla) when the quietness of the morning was shuttered by a big commotion. Clueless for a few long moments I wondered if the soldiers were coming to kill us. Soon though, once my mind recovered from the shock, I realized it was just another fight between the two brothers. Both yelled and swore at the top of their voices and slammed the bamboo sticks each held on the side wall of the house in clearly fruitless attempts to scare the other. Khala, who had come out to inquire, was frantic. "Stop! Stop! Are you boys out of your minds?"

Moni bhai, bloodshot eyes and dry mouth from all the shouting, howled over her.

"This idiot is an agent of India. He wants to hold hands with Awami league. We are Muslims, we must hang with Muslims. Pakistanis are brothers. We need to shoot agents like you to death..." The last part was aimed at Roni bhai, to everybody's relief.

Roni bhai wasn't going to lose in this shouting match, not without a fight. "Shut up you suck up of the Pakistanis." He shouted back. "They neither feed us nor shelter us. Why should we stay with them? Sheikh Mujib is right. No co-operation with them anymore. Enough is enough."

At this point both banged on the wall several times to make their points. Khala had had just enough. She chased the boys. "Are you boys trying to break the house? Go somewhere else if you must fight. You are not damaging my wall."

"Get out! Get out!" The parrot joined in.

Khalu had just settled in his chamber with a cup of tea. He hoped to check out quickly the case load of the day. All these noise must have had a less than desirable effect on him because he came galloping with his sleepers in his hands. He gave both the brothers a few smacks. None of them cared much but returned the favour by losing their sticks and wrestling away to the street.

Khalu threw his sleepers in front of Yunus. "Go on. See if the cobbler is there. "

I went along with Yunus. I really loved to watch the cobbler sewing the shoes and sleepers. There was a nice rhythm to it. I wasn't really dreaming to become a cobbler when I grew up but wished to buy the equipments and try the art secretly at home.

Most days the supper dragged to midnight. Heavy afternoon snacks were customary resulting into no appetite until late at night. In addition, khalu regularly retired from his chamber late, often juggling his time with the case load and political agendas. A few days after the rumble between the brothers khalu looked anxious during supper time. Usually he ate silently and didn't say anything unless spoken to. Today was an exception. The brothers were about to restart their perennial argument about Awami league and Muslim league in between munching their mouth full of food when khalu rebuffed them strongly. "Listen all, time is bad. Yahya and Mujib were unable to reach an agreement. Lots of Pakistani soldiers are coming here. Watch out when you speak. Having political difference is not unusual but that doesn't mean you have to act on that."

"We are not afraid of them." Roni bhai strongly said. "We'll grab Yahya by the neck and throw the bugger into the trash. Bastard!"

"Shut up...." Moni bhai shouted back sputtering mouth full of rice all around him.

Khalu snapped. "Don't fight like kids. Nobody knows how the situation turns. Remember, family is above everything. Don't fight among brothers. Siblings are the dearest of all."

In this grave moment the crazy parrot called out, "Hello beauty!"

Khalu looked mad. "Why doesn't somebody kick this stupid bird away?"

"Innocent bird, why blame it?" Khala said. "It's Yunus who taught it to talk like that."

Khalu looked around for Yunus. He had already fled out of there.

Waking up next morning I found Yunus mournful. I knew something was seriously wrong. He silently pointed out the empty cage of the parrot. So, beauty had escaped. Who knew how? Yunus and I went out to look for the parrot. We searched all over the town with no luck. I had never before seen Yunus shading tears, didn't think he was even capable of.

On this day he knelt down on the ground, hid his face between his knees and cried like a little baby.

Chapter 8

After the speech by Sheikh Mujibur Rahman on 7th March nobody had any doubt that the situation was quickly turning into trouble. Mujibur Rahman had declared loudly and clearly, "Our stand is for freedom. Our stand is for independence." Kids of tender age were obsessed by such speeches. Many of us would repeat the whole speech word by word at any opportunity we got. One time I got severely scolded by Moni bhai for doing so. A supporter of Muslim league he believed in united Pakistan. Roni bhai had a completely different standing. He wanted independent Bangladesh. He was angry and complained about the way things were going. Why didn't Mujib declared war on 7th March? What was the meaning of attempting to fix something that had no chances? Bastard Yahya Khan! Bastard Tikka Khan! They had no business in this country and needed to be booted without delay.

Naturally the frequency in which two of them got into arguments increased alarmingly after Mujib's speech. Some even worried that the two brothers might try to battle it out long before the two Pakistan did.

There were some signs of ensuing devastation but nobody even imagined how heinous it would turn out to be. On March 25, 1971, in the dark of the night the Pakistani soldiers attacked the peaceful, self-righteous inhabitants of Dhaka. Their main targets were Dhaka University and Old Dhaka. They attacked the EPR base located in Pilkhana without any warning. Iqbal hall - one of the residential halls located in Dhaka university - was the headquarter of the freedom minded young men and became the primary target of the West Pakistani soldiers. A little after midnight the calmness of Dhaka was shuttered in the deadly firings of mortars and machineguns. The rushing blood of the dead and the final cries of the wounded filled the air of the city. The attackers then lighted the Nilkhet slum and when the helpless slum dwellers tried to escape from the deadly flame they shot them mercilessly. Jogannath and several other student resident halls were also attacked simultaneously. Once the main attack subsided the soldiers entered the student halls and in a display of most barbaric attitude shot and killed the students who were holed up inside the compounds.

When all these were happening I slept in peace. Rushi and I used to sleep beside mom. After an active day once the supper settled into my stomach I blacked out for the night. Even Rushi, a habitual bad sleeper who frequently moved all over the bed and rested her legs on me, could not bother me. Lately mom looked really embarrassing with her belly turning even bigger than ever. She had to visit the bathroom several times at night. Each of her visits caused a mini earthquake in the house. Even that wasn't enough to wake me up. However, on 25th March, all the chaos that started around dawn was enough to make an exception. The streets seemed to liven up in grief and anger. I heard Roni bhai shouting at the top of his voice. "Those bastards think they can shoot us all dead. We'll fight for independence. Wake up everybody. Listen to the radio. The sons of the bitches are drowning Dhaka in our blood. Get up all."

Any other time Moni bhai would have yelled back at him for waking everybody up in the middle of the night, but today he was totally absent from action. I sensed khala and khalu waking up. Still quite sleepy I dragged myself up in a sitting position. Mom whispered to me, "Sleep baby. You don't need to know this. Not yet."

I didn't object. I was too sleepy to give in to the curiosity. I didn't even know when I went back to sleep.

As I opened my eyes a shiny sunlit day welcomed me. Stepping out of the room I knew something horrible had happened. The door of khalu's chamber was tightly closed. We could hear loud arguments inside. There were many voices but unlike other days I could barely hear khalu. I found Moni bhai sitting quietly on the porch. Roni bhai was nowhere to be seen. Khala was making flat bread as she did every morning. A woman from the nearby slum came to help her in house works. She was known as Parvoti's mom. Hindu by religion, she wore sindur (vermilion) on her forehead. She used to roll the flat breads while khala baked them on a flat pan.

Smell of the freshly baked breads filled the air. I peeked into the kitchen.

"Hungry?" Khala asked.

I nodded.

"Wait a bit. I am frying some cauliflower. It would taste good with flat bread."

I patiently waited on the veranda. Moni bhai looked grave and grumpy, totally unapproachable. I stood by the grilled window and looked down to observe the daily chores of the slum next to the pond. Interestingly even there things looked different, grave to some degree. They had gathered in small groups and discussed in low voices. Even the toddlers with running noses stood by silently sucking their thumbs. My curiosity rose sky high. I gave another side look at Moni bhai and decided for the second time not to risk bothering him. I had no desire to get scolded so early in the morning. Suddenly Yunus bolted in from the streets.

"Do you have any idea what happened last night?" He wearily said. "Pakistani soldiers killed many people. They took away Sheikh Mujib. Now they are going to regret it. We are going to hit back with maximum force. They don't know the Bengalis."

I knew he was going to get it.

"Shut up, you idiot." Moni bhai snapped at him. "What do you know? This is the result of conspiracy by the Hindus. They want to break down the unity of the Muslims. They want to make this land another kingdom for the Hindus. Good that a few Hindu bastards were killed. All of them should be killed."

I have never seen Yunus speaking up on anybody in this household. Today he must have been possessed.

"What are you saying, Moni bhai?" He quickly responded. "Did you hear what they said on the radio? They killed Muslims mostly. Do you know how many students were killed in Dhaka University? I know I am an uneducated idiot. I barely understand all this. But you do, don't you? Do you think these killings were good? Muslims killing Muslims?"

For a moment it seemed that Moni bhai was about to burst into anger but he struggled to contain himself. "This is what happens when you hold hands with the bastard Hindus." He muttered, almost illegibly.

Parvoti's mom had worked in this house for many years. I barely heard her ever talking more than a few words. "Chachi, why is Moni bhai so mad at us?" She mildly objected from the kitchen. "What did we do? This is our country too. What sin did we do by taking birth as Hindus? This is the religion of our ancestors. "

"Let it go." Khala said. "Don't take it seriously. This is all political talk. You know Moni since he was a little boy. Don't listen to all this crap."

"All Hindus should go back to the Hindu kingdom of India. Bangladesh is the country of Muslims," muttered Moni bhai before thumping his way out.

Parvoti's mom started to sob. Khala tried to soothe her.

"Don't listen to Moni bhai." Yunus whispered in my ears. "He doesn't want freedom. He likes to do slavery of the bastard Pakistanis. They are nothing but sons of bitches. Muslim - my foot!"

I knew Yunus had become a protégé of Roni bhai. "Where's Roni bhai?" I asked.

"In the school ground." Yunus whispered. "Many have gathered there. We are going to fight. We can't keep quiet anymore. Do you want to come with me?"

I nodded. I knew mom and khala would try to stop me, so we tried to slip out secretly but to no avail. Rushi saw me. Immediately mom came screaming out. "Khoka, don't go out of the house."

I was old enough to know no good could come from breaking such direct command. When angry, mom was capable of making things quite uncomfortable with her barrage of slaps, pinches and hair pulling. Yunus read my mind. He shrugged and promised to take me another time.

"Yunus, where are you going?" Khala called out.

"I'll be back in a minute."

"I didn't ask when you'll be back. Where are you going?"

Yunus had already slipped out.

On 26th March from the radio center of Chittagong Major Ziaur Rahman announced the declaration of independence on behalf of the provisional government of Bangladesh. This created a huge wave of commotions in the country. Most greeted it with joy and enthusiasm. Waves of people flooded the streets announcing solidarity with the provisional government.

The heat was felt clearly inside khala's house as well. Naturally, Khalu and Moni bhai were under immense pressure. They remained quiet, cautious. On the other hand Roni bhai romped around in support of the war. Many wanted to join the war but had no battle training whatsoever. The possibility of setting up training facilities in this side of the border looked bleak. Roni bhai and his friends planned to make the trip to India. We heard many had already gone to India to train with firearms.

Khala broke down at this news. Mom tried to talk Roni bhai out of it, unsuccessfully. Even Yunus was all set to go with him. However, under pressure from several fronts he eventually backed away. At the end Roni bhai quietly left for India with a few of his close friends. Moni bhai continued to have small gatherings in the den on the roof but he could barely hide his anxiousness. It was one thing to support Muslim league and another to oppose the independence of your own land. From their discussion it was easy to make out that they were confused. Sometimes when they didn't have enough partners Moni bhai allowed me to play cards with them. I took this opportunity to pick up a few games. Roni bhai came up frequently in their discussions.

"Eh, what a warrior! He'll pass away in one slap on the face." Moni bhai often muttered in disgust.

It was quite clear that the sudden fame that Roni bhai gained had made him jealous. Even some of the pretty girls in the neighbourhood had stopped me to ask about Roni bhai, inquiring to know if he had really gone to join the war. In my mind I had no doubt that when Roni bhai returned from war he would have no problem getting one of these pretty damsels.

We received another letter from dad soon after. They had received the news of the barbaric events of 25th March but did not get the true picture. The radio centers in West Pakistan had presented the news in a way as if the West Pakistan military had only captured a few conspirators. During their operations some Hindus might have met their ends. The number of East Pakistani soldiers in dad's regiment was only about 5%. Most of them were doctors. Their main task was to accompany the Pakistani soldiers to different engagements and treat them for sickness and injuries. They continued their duties despite the declaration of Independence of Bangladesh. They weren't quite sure what role they needed to play. Confused and worried they performed their respective tasks. Dad was very anxious to see us. He hadn't found any housing for us yet. His anxiety was so overwhelming that finally in desperation he decided to meet General Gul, who was the superior authority of the Quetta cantonment. He would be able to help him, dad believed. Mom read the letter infinite times and cried relentlessly. I wasn't sure what all the crying was about. There was no way she could even make the trip to Quetta in her current size and shape.

In the meantime like an added trouble arrived my toothache. I had sweet teeth from very early age. Lozenges were my inseparable company. Often I forgot to brush or floss. As a result my milk teeth were mostly destroyed by cavity. My broad smile used to make even the most serious person chuckle. Such clownish was my appearance. When several teeth started to hurt like hell and gave me sleepless nights I had no other option but to resort to the least popular solution – visiting a dentist. One fine day it was decided that we would visit the dental clinic of Asfaq chacha.

A very big man Asfaq chacha was dad's second cousin. Just looking at him could make a kid run away. Many times I had wondered how a man with such large stature managed to walk around doing regular chores. Our planned visit to him must have imprinted sign of anxiety on my face because even mom felt the need to put up some kind words. "What's there to be scared of? He really likes you."

"What liking has anything to do with extracting teeth?" I muttered.

Mom laughed. "How many times did I tell you to brush properly? Now you'll have to face the consequences."

"Cavity boy!" Rushi giggled. I glared at her.

I would have given her a smack on the head but had to pull myself back. It would be a bad idea in mom's presence. We were to visit Asfaq chacha in the evening. My heart started to beat faster. I couldn't concentrate on anything and spent most of the day lying down on bed.

Asfaq chacha's clinic was in the first floor of a two storied building located at the corner of the block known as Dak Bangla. He allowed himself a broad smile at my very sight. "How are you doing, son? You succeeded in destroying most of your teeth, haven't you? Don't worry. These are all milk teeth. You'll get nice new teeth once these are gone."

All these pep talk didn't make me feel better for a second. Asfaq chacha had me seated on a high dental chair and examined my teeth. Every now and then he mumbled, "Exactly what I thought. This one is totally gone. That one doesn't look very good either. You need to cut down on lozenges."

"I keep telling him. He wouldn't listen." Mom spread some salt on the open wound.

After his examination concluded Asfaq chacha gave up a big smile, which totally freaked me out. "Nothing to worry! For now I'll just take out the two teeth that are hurting you. If you are still in pain come back. I'll take care of the rest."

He smilingly picked up a gigantic syringe. "Just need to put your gums to sleep."

I saw total darkness for a few seconds, mostly out of fear. The actual experience turned out to be nowhere as painful as I was anticipating. He quickly uprooted the two teeth, folded them in a piece of paper and handed them over to me. Mom had almost no money with her but she still offered him the regular fee. He refused to take it. "Sis, I can't take money from you." He smilingly added. "I'll take it from his dad when I see him again. If the boy is having any other issues just bring him back. Don't be shy. I haven't done much for them. This way I can feel a little less guilty."

I tried to hide my worries. I had no desire to head back this way again – painful or pain free. Nevertheless I had to revisit him twice more that month. He merrily pulled out half of my teeth. When the ordeal was over he patted on my back and smilingly said," Take care of your teeth. Next time I'll pull all the rest."

I feared the gigantic syringe. Returning home I brushed and flossed several times for a few days before the lapses started to happen. Sensing my degrading motivation mom put Rushi on my back. This strained our sibling relationship further but worked. I would do just about anything to make Rushi quiet.

Chapter 9

A few days later we received an urgent message about jhima. She wasn't doing well. She had been suffering from varieties of health issues for ages and went through ups and downs but rarely anything life threatening. A man who had come to Khulna from village for personal reasons carried the message. He mentioned with great details how vulnerable jhima had become mentally and physically and demanded to see me particularly. Mom wasn't in any condition to travel. She had difficulties just to go to the bathroom. Yet she told the man to let dadu know that if he sent somebody for us we would go. Who knew when death would strike? This could be our last opportunity to see jhima one more time.

Dadu himself came to get us the very next day after he got the message. We learned from him that jhima was bed ridden. Her body had swollen and she could barely move. She wasn't in a condition to eat or drink normally and everybody feared that her last moment was nearing quickly. She had been constantly asking to see me. We knew it was against our best judgement to drag mom into this trip to the village but everybody bowed out to her determination and we were on our way the following morning.

The regular bus service between Khulna and Satkhira wasn't operational due to some kind of labour unrest. We were forced to ride scooters, rick-shaws and even walked some before reaching Kali-gonj after dusk. Mom was totally exhausted but she tried her best to hide it. After crossing the river we found Alek waiting for us with his bullock cart and a mouthful of smile. Once on the cart mom collapsed on her back. With every movement of the cart she grumbled in pain. Comically Rushi echoed mom grumble by grumble. Alek and I burst into giggles. When was she going to get in her senses? Dadu had left his bike in a store in Kaligonj on his way to Khulna. He picked it up and rode it slowly beside the cart trying to stay with it. He looked worried for mom and inquired about her condition every few minutes. "How are you feeling now, dear? We are almost there."

As we advanced slowly Alek Mia took the liberty to sing out loudly a familiar rural song "Oh, the lonely boat..."

Dadu instantly shut him down. "Alek, keep your mouth closed."

Alek turned completely quiet. Dadu was known for his terrible temper. Everybody played it safely around him. With his permission I slipped out of the cover and sat by Alek at the front. Alek passed on the thin stick that he was carrying to me. "Go on; drive the cows for a little bit. Don't hit them hard. They can feel pain."

There were two oxen – one red and one black – pulling the cart. I gave a very soft tap on the back of the red coloured ox. "Let's go, come on!"

It turned its neck and gave me a tender look. "This ox belongs to you." Alek said. "Jhima gave it to you. And this black ox belongs to your dadu."

It took me by surprise. "This red one is mine?"

"Yes. Jhima has three other cows. One of them is a female. She is pregnant again. Jhima says when she dies you'll get everything that she owns. She practically raised you since you were born. She has unconditional love for you. Don't ever hurt her, okay?"

I already knew jhima had special bonding with me. What I didn't know was the fact that I had an ox, a red one! My heart filled with joy. The ownership of such a big and beautiful living thing seemed over-whelming. "Alek bhai, don't hit it too hard, okay?" I pledged.

Alek laughed. "Why would I hit it, dear? I just poke them a little bit to keep them moving. They are innocent animal, I'll never hurt them."

His laughter echoed in the calm and quiet sur-roundings of the nightfall. Dadu looked annoyed. "Keep your mouth closed, Alek." He gravely said.

"Yes, chaca." Alek muttered, apologetically.

Seconds later he glanced at me stealthily and blinked.

At dadu's house we were greeted by a large crowd, larger than I had ever remembered seeing. The news of jhima approaching her last moments had spread quickly and many of our relatives had made the trip to see her for the last time. There was barely any space in the courtyard. The place shone brightly with the lights from several powerful lamps. Our presence generated a loud buzz with everybody rushing forward to take a peek at us. Several voices called out with garbled words. The only one that I could recognize belonged to Shahid chacha. He kept on repeating himself. "Khoka is here! Khoka is here! Open your eyes, jhima, your khoka is here. Move away! Move away!"

Mom, Rushi and I moved through the crowd and climbed up on the porch of jhima's hut. She was inside her room lying down on the floor over a handmade carpet. Beside her sat anxiously the village allopathic and the ayurvedic (an ancient healing practice from India) doctors.

Her body was swollen almost beyond recognition, eyes closed. When Shahid chacha announced our presence she opened her eyes, her murky vision roamed around aimlessly, showed no sign of remembering any of us.

Mom almost collapsed by her side, totally drained after the stressful long trip. "Jhima, wake up. Look, khoka is here. Can you hear me?"

None of us noticed when chachu stood by us. "Jhima hasn't been talking since noon. Go on khoka, sit by her side for a little bit."

I did as told. That didn't do any magic. Jhima lied down on the floor with her eyes closed like a corpse. Looking around I noticed with surprise that not only Minu apa had come from Satkhira but also came nana and several others form maternal side. At the sight of nana mom suddenly lost all her resistance and broke into tears. Nana hugged her and patted her, speaking soothingly. "Don't worry. Everything will be okay. You should rest."

Mom howled. Any other time this would be pretty embarrassing but for the time being it wasn't totally out of place. And then I saw Rani apa in the crowd with mama and fupi. She waved at me. I waved back with a big smile. I was already feeling much better.

That night none of us got much sleep. Most people slept on the courtyard on handmade carpets. The weather was warm with no rain. Nobody complained. We – Rushi, Rani Apa, Minu Apa and I slept in dadi's bed. Rushi was knocked out in moments. The three of us stayed awake quite late whispering under the sheet to avoid attracting undue attention. I didn't even know when I dozed off.

Next morning when I woke up the sun was already high in the sky. I noticed the crowd had lightened. I climbed down to the courtyard and found a small crowd in front of jhima's hut. Pushing through the crowd I saw both Minu apa and Rani apa patiently sitting on the floor. Minu apa waved at me. "Jhima is well now." She sounded excited. "Since morning she could sit on her own and has been making conversation. Come, she has been asking for you."

Jhima was lying down on her back, eyes closed, still very weak. She must have sensed my presence because she slowly opened her eyes. Her lips extended in a pale smile. "Khoka! When did you come? Come to me. All the kids, come, sit by my sides. "

We hugged her tenderly and sat by her quietly for a while. She wasn't in a condition to talk much but she wept silently with tears running down her cheek.

"Why are you crying?" Rani apa wiped off the tears. "You are okay now."

"Allah spared me this time just for the kids." Jhima whispered. "What else do I have to live for?"

Most visitors left that afternoon. The caravan of bullock carts parked in front of the outhouse disappeared one by one until only one was left. This was nana's cart. Allah must have had listened to my silent prayers because soon we learned that while nana with junior and senior nani would return to Dorgahpur Rani apa and her parents would stay a few more days. Alek would drop them later. This was something to celebrate for, especially when I found out even Minu apa and her parents were staying back for a few more days. This was getting better and better.

It was summer time and the mango trees scattered all over my grandparent's property had fruited profusely. There were several varieties each with its specialty – East Indian. Florigon, Glenn, Imam Pasand, Mallika, Neelum, Edward, Bombay, Alphonso, Cushman. They came in all shapes and sizes and had distinct tastes, textures and flavour. Several of the trees were grafted and produced the best fruits. Most mangoes had local names to quickly identify them. Two of our favourite ones were 'Kacha-mitha' (green and sweet) and 'Kolop' (grafted plant). The mangoes had just started to ripen, some varieties more than the rest. We always targeted 'kacha-mitha' mangoes first for its fibreless flesh and the delicious taste that had the touch of both sweetness and bit tanginess. They were usually large when matured. The problem was this tree was very tall, almost like an adult coconut tree. None of us could climb this tree and resorted to throwing rocks or pellets in our futile attempt to drop some of the fruits. The tree produced few mangoes and they were usually at the top of the tree. We had to ask for Alek's help. He was a master climber who was expert in scaling coconut trees. I had seen very few people who could scale vertical length so deftly. If he could spare some time he climbed up the 'kacha-mitha' tree and got us a few mangoes. We peeled them, cut them into small pieces and mixed them up with salt, milk, lemon leaf and chilli. We devoured it often fighting for larger share.

The pond in the backyard had a huge mango tree leaning over it. This one had small yellow fruits. When bathing in the pond we threw pellets to drop the mangoes. When one fell we competed to grab it first. The 'Kolop' tree was located on the other side of the pond, near the small family grave where dadu's parents were buried. This tree produced large mangoes with beautiful green and red hue. This was a small tree but bore so many mangoes that the branches leaned in the weight of the fruits. These mangoes didn't taste very well when green but was something to die for as it ripened. We had already noticed some of them were ripening.

A few days later one afternoon dark cloud rolled in and covered the sky. People anxiously wrapped up whatever they were doing, moved dry stuff indoor, drove the brood of chickens and ducks in their coup, closed the doors and finally took shelter inside the house. "There's going to be a tropical storm." Rani apa said. "The mangoes will drop like hails."

"Really!" This was news to me. "Are we going to pick them?"

The answer came from chachi. "I don't want to see anybody going out during the storm." She warned rather sternly.

We restrained from responding. When the mangoes would be dropping how could anybody possibly stay home? Who had ever heard of such impossible thing? Especially in the villages not only the kids but even the adults dared the storm to pick fallen mangoes, Rani apa educated me. It was of a big concern to us that the opportunists might rush to the garden first and picked up the desired ones before we had a chance. We waited patiently for chachi to move away to help others preparing for the storm and concocted a secret plan. We anxiously observed the progression of the storm hoping that it would blew on us before it was too late at night. If we dozed off the others might beat us to the chase.

The sky turned darker and darker by the minute. Even the wind stopped blowing. The domestic hands hurriedly returned to their homes. My uncles and aunts gathered in grandpa's room prepared to pass the storm there. We kids took shelter in jhima's hut along with mom. We huddled with jhima in the king size bed she slept on. Due to the oncoming storm we had eaten our supper early. Alek had driven the cattle in the shed long ago, ate his supper and took shelter in the outhouse. He alternatively went back home or slept here at night. Today dadi had specifically asked him to stay back. If the cattle felt distressed during the storm he would come very handy. We had stopped by in the outhouse to see him once. He had spread out a handmade carpet and was preparing to sleep. After spending whole day on the fields he used to get very tired by dusk. I had seen him gobbling up a large plate filled with rice and then go to bed directly.

Tonight we had given him an added responsibility. During the storm children from the neighbouring houses came out to pick mangoes. While some of them were from well-off families a majority belonged to families who were poor. Even though there were so many fruit trees in the villages many of these poor people had very little access to those. Tropical storms gave them an opportunity to grab a few fruits. Alek's job was to shout to keep them away. Once we were done they could pick to their hearts content. This was our garden and we felt we should get the priority.

Hunkered down inside jhima's hut we chatted on to keep us engaged and awake, our eyes and ears focused outside. The storm seemed to take awfully long to hit us. Rani apa called out for Alek every few minutes to ensure that he didn't fell asleep. Initially he was responding but as the night deepened we stopped hearing from him. Rani apa was upset. "Great! He fell asleep. Why the stupid storm isn't here yet?"

"Sleep." Jhima urged. "Who knows when the storm would come?"

After struggling to keep awake for another half an hour we finally gave up and went to sleep. There was little chance the storm was coming tonight. After running around whole day I was pretty tired and probably was the first one to fall asleep.

Suddenly I was shaken out of my sleep. Rani Apa stood by my side, all ready to go. "Get up." She said, boiling in excitement. "The storm is here. Can you hear the mangoes dropping?"

I was tired and had to force myself to get up. However, soon the excitement captured me as well and I jumped out of the bed, slid the sleepers into my feet and was already to venture out. I could hear the wind blowing forcefully. We opened one of the doors slightly and slipped out into the courtyard. It was dark and I could barely see my own hands. Minu apa grabbed a flashlight and lead us through the back-door into the garden. Jhima was a light sleeper. The blasting of the wind against the walls and trees must have had woken her up. She called out to stop us but to no avail. We heard the mangoes dropping constantly, almost like rocks falling from the sky. There was no stopping now.

We fought the strong wind and ubiquitous dust on our way through the garden. We had to cover our eyes with the palm of our hands to save them from the gust and flying debris. We could hear the voices of other people nearby. Clearly many had already beaten us to it. Desperation and anger both flashed through my mind. We started to run ignoring the turmoil that was happening around. Our first destination was 'Green and sweet' tree. Rani Apa was carrying a large jute bag.

To our relief there were only a handful of people under this tree. We knelt down on the ground and looked as several flashlights danced around. We found fewer than we expected. Annoyed Rani apa even tried to drive the visitors away. The wind blew so hard that we could barely hear us standing next to each other. It wasn't clear if the intruders heard her or not but they continued their search. We did not want to spend too much time there and moved to our next primary target, the 'Kalap' tree. That tree had a superb fruiting and naturally most would rush there hoping to pick many. We again dared the strong wind roaring at us and walked by the backyard pond to the 'Kalap' tree. Minu apa stayed ahead and focused her flashlight on the trail as Rani apa and I almost flanked her.

Our fear proved to be true. When we reached the tree we found several older girls had already gathered there. We competed with them to pick up as many as we could. Rani apa again shouted at them a few times to discourage them. But they didn't pay much attention. In any case, soon our bag was full. I still continued to pick and shoved them into the large pockets of my shorts. The storm seemed to pick up speed. We shouted at each other to ensure that we didn't separate. I could hear chacha and chachi calling out for us. "Let's go back." Minu apa shouted. "Dad and mom found out. We are into lot of trouble. "

We had to head back, which turned out to be more difficult now with the heavy sack filled with mangoes. Three of us dragged it slowly careful not to lose any. Finally when we struggled our way back to the house we were greeted by chachi who looked very much mad. She berated us mercilessly. The good part was we didn't even hear most of it because of the roaring wind. We carried the mango sack inside jhima's hut and counted the mangoes. Total eighty five. Not bad. We smiled with satisfaction.

Next morning we woke up early and went back to the garden. The storm subsided long ago. In the dark our vision was limited and we missed out many. In the day light we found several more mangoes that went unnoticed by everybody. At the end we had collected more than one hundred and fifty. However, we didn't keep all the mangoes. Not all were good to eat. When mom heard about our night venture she turned quite mad as well. However, when we prepared the 'Green and sweet' mangoes with salt and spices and offered her a generous portion she was all smile and licked the last bit of it. "Did you kids pick up these mangoes last night? Not bad at all." There was sign of admiration in her voice. This was something new for me. I frowned. How about considering that before going ballistic? Who wanted to be embarrassed in front of the whole household?

Minu Apa and her family left couple of days later. The war had started. Even though the impact wasn't yet noticeable in our region but they didn't feel comfortable to stay away from home for too long. Who knew how the things would turn? I heard that many people from the neighbouring villages had signed up for the war and went to India for training. Indian border was only two - three miles away.

It was a common fear that the war would turn bigger and bloodier. India hadn't yet expressed its support directly but was helping in various ways. Many people trying to escape the brutality of war had left Bangladesh and entered the Indian Territory. India had to make shelter for those refugees. They were also helping the freedom fighters with battle-field training. Moti bhai, Alek's older brother, had joined the war and went to India for training. Rohim and Liakot worked as day labourer for dadu. They had gone with Moti bhai as well. Though there was contrasting opinions among the villagers but we heard that some people were doing horrible things in the name of the war. Some were even engaged in robbing houses of the rich farmers. Rani apa believed that Bashir had joined a team of robbers. She was scared. Who knew what was Bashir planning to do? She had no choice but to tell mama everything about Bashir. Since then Mama wouldn't let her go alone anywhere. He also bought a rifle. But could a single rifle save them against a heinous gang?

After Minu apa left Rani apa and I had little more time to discuss some personal issues. I felt her deep anxiety about Bashir. I was angry with the fact that a twelve year old girl like her had to be worried about such things. Looking at her I failed to see anything that may interest an adult. Why would a young man like Bashir come after just a girl like her? Rani apa smiled when I asked her.

"You know nothing about the village life." She answered bitterly. "There are so many girls of my age who are forced into marriage now. By the time they are seventeen they are mother of two. That's the tradition here. I'll get out of here. I already asked dad to send me to Khulna. Who knows how the situation would turn in the village as the war continues? You must know how difficult it is for woman during the war times. Not only the enemies but even the compatriots become formidable. They are left with no place to go."

I sat silently for a long time with a sore heart. I didn't yet understand the concept of war fully. I didn't even know clearly why there was a war being fought between East and West Pakistan but just the thought of Rani apa being harmed got me filled with both anger and distress.

Within a few days jhima started to feel much better. She started to walk around using her stick. Not everybody in the household welcomed that though. One of her shortcomings was to pick on others at every possible opportunity. Not only the servants but even dadi was afraid of her sharp tongue. When she was bedridden everybody felt a little relaxed. But as soon as she started to walk around the household with her stick things turned a little uncomfortable. However, jhima seemed to have a change of heart. To everybody's amazement she ignored most and spent majority of the day with me and Rani apa. After Alek took the cattle to the fields in the morning three of us would walk to the vegetable garden outside the courtyard. As we picked vegetables we talked about many things. I had no clue that jhima had such a rich collection of stories in her stock. Most of her stories were about the kings and landlords, some were quite scary. Especially the story she told us about the pond in the backyard gave me nightmares for several nights.

A few generations before our ancestral house weren't located here. Instead a heinous dacoit named Bishnu lived here. During day time he was a good farmer who spent time cultivating the small amount of land that he had. His wife Sulekha was a simple woman who loved her husband dearly. She was very devoted to him. BIshnu loved her as well. At least that's what everybody thought. But Bishnu was a good actor. He changed his nice personality at night and robbed the rich farmers of their valuables.

Every month he robbed one household with his army of robbers. With their giant knives when they broke into the houses of the rich farmers there was nothing they could do but panic. Bishnu would command them to put all their jewellery and golden coins in a sack. If anybody objected he slaughtered them. After sharing the loot with his gang members Bishnu took his portion and put it in large round clay pots and stored them in an underground storage. When the pot became full he closed the mouth tightly and sunk it in the pond. That way even if anybody ever suspected him they couldn't possibly find any evidence. Bishnu's plan was to have four or five such pots full with valuables and then pick them all up secretly, move to another place and buy lots of lands to become a landlord.

He had never shared any of this with his wife Sulekha but she was becoming suspicious. Sometimes when she woke up at night she didn't find her husband by her side. When asked Bishnu would say he couldn't sleep so just went for a walk by the river. Sulekha had hard time believing that. One time after a robbery Bishnu hid his loot inside the secret underground storage and found himself face to face to his wife as he walked out. Left with no other option he shared the secret with his wife. However, he also cautioned her that if anybody knew anything about it he would kill her.

Sulekha loved her husband but she also feared him equally. Especially now that she knew about this totally new and fearsome side of her husband she was truly scared. Terrified that something may slip out her mouth mistakenly and put her in danger she even stopped going out of the house. Bishnu continued to rob without any trouble. His fifth pot was about to be filled. He decided that he would rob only one more house. He picked a well off farmer who lived far away from his home and broke into his house with his gang in the middle of the night. However, unlike other times, o when he saw the unmarried young and beautiful daughter of the landlord he totally lost his mind. This time not only valuables but on his way out he also tied down the girl and brought her with him. Sulekha rolled her eyes and objected.

"This girl will stay with us." Bishnu declared. "I'll marry her."

"How can you take another wife when you already have one?" Sulekha bitterly demanded.

"I did not think about that." Bishnu thoughtfully said. "Okay. I'll return her tomorrow. Let's hide her in the underground storage for just tonight."

Sulekha felt relieved. But Bishnu had another plan. Next day during meal he secretly mixed up poison into his wife's food. After consuming that poison Sulekha lost consciousness. Bishnu tied her up with his fifth pot and sunk it in the pond. His plan was to marry the other girl first, then when the proper opportunity came bring up the pots out of the water, carry them to a distant village, buy a few hundred acres of lands and build a palace. Even though he had snatched the girl away, once they got married she would have no choice but to accept her fate, he thought.

As planned he forced the girl into marrying him. Everybody learned that Sulekha had lost her mind and went away without telling anybody anything. Bishnu stopped robbing and looked around for a suitable village to settle in.

Finally, one night he dipped in the pond to pick up his clay pots with valuables. After picking up the first four pots and placing them by the side of the pond he went to get the fifth one. The pot still had the corpse of his wife tied to it. The corpse had started to rot. Bishnu tried to untie the rope and separate the pot from the corpse but to his amazement the long saree that Sulekha wore suddenly came at him like a snake and coiled around him. The more he tried to swim up the more it pulled him down. After struggling for sometime Bishnu could no longer hold his breath and slowly died. Next morning people found the four pots on the side of the pond but even after searching thoroughly inside the pond they neither found the corpse of Bishnu and Sulekha nor the fifth pot filled with valuables. But the legend went that the pot rose above the water randomly with Sulekha's corpse tied to it and at length floated Bishnu's corpse coiled in Sulekha's saree. *Anybody who would see that view would die exactly in one week.*

After hearing this story I totally stopped going to the backyard pond. Especially after dusk I avoided the vicinity completely.

A few days later Rani apa left too. We were under a lot of confusion. Mom hadn't been doing very well. I heard that the baby who was growing inside her belly was scheduled to come out soon.

Would it be a wise decision for her to get into another trip to Khulna? The situation in the rural areas
wasn't that bad yet. So why not wait until the baby
was born? Dadu, dadi and jhima reasoned to con-
vince mom. Mom must have had plans to go to her
sister's house and have the baby born there but at
the end she bowed to her poor physical condition
and decided to stay back in the village.

We hadn't received any more news from dad
either. We had no way to know how he was doing in
Pakistan. As the possibility of joining with him kept
on pushed back mom became more and more mel-
ancholy. I could sense her agony. Even I felt quite a
bit of anger on dad for taking so long to have the
family reunited.

Chapter 10

Only about a week had passed by since Rani apa had left. Jhima had been healthy and returned to her normal routine of pestering everybody with her usual manners. Mom wasn't doing any better. She spent most of her time on her back. Rushi and I spent a lot of time in the vegetable gardens with dadi, helping her picking varieties of vegetables and fruits. It wasn't very exciting but I wasn't particularly bored, especially considering the fact that since mom was bedridden I was saved from all the scolding that was due every day. I was savouring these moments. Jhima told me that after the baby was born mom would be limited in movement for at least a month or two. This meant I would be enjoying my freedom even longer than I anticipated. Unfortunately my happiness was very short.

One night my dadu's house was breached by a group of dacoits. The house was secured by almost eight feet high walls made of mud and bamboo sticks. The main house, kitchen, outhouse, Jhima's hut and the cattle shed everything was inside the walls. They had four wooden grain storages (gola) all of which were located on the yard between the main house and the outhouse. Every day after dusk when the cattle was driven inside the shed, the main door was tightly closed by bolts and extra strength log placed across the door (hoorko). Once the poultry moved into their coup the back door was bolted and secured by a hoorko as well. The domestic helps returned to their homes before it was dark. Time was not good and things turned very quiet after dusk. The fear of thieves and dacoits had increased drastically.

Many years back dadu's house was robbed once. Overall situation of the countryside was not very good. Many did not have food to survive. The dacoits took the grains from his storage, did not harm anybody. Police were informed. Nobody ever was apprehended. Even though dadu was well off today but he wasn't so rich that the dacoits would be interested in robbing him. Their main target was cash money and jewellery. Dadu had much land but practically no cash. Dadi and jhima had a handful of gold jewellery. Nobody ever thought dacoits would care to take the trouble to get those measly valuables.

That night after supper we hit the bed in between eight and nine. I was listening to jhima telling me some more stories and didn't know when I fell asleep. Suddenly there was a loud noise and I jumped out of the bed. Jhima had waken up about the same time. We could clearly hear four or five male voices roaring in the courtyard. "Hey old haggard, open the door." Somebody shouted. "Step outside. Now!"

I heard dadu's door opening. Dadu slowly walked out in the porch. He was holding a hurricane. In the pale light he looked weak, helpless. I peeked through the narrow gaps of the wooden door and saw the yard was flooded in light from several powerful flashlights. A few men with their faces covered in a thin towel (gamcha) were walking up and down the courtyard restlessly. One of them approached dadu in long and strong strides. He was probably the leader of this group. "Get me all the money and jewellery that you have in the house." He said coarsely. "You have ten minutes. If you don't comply I am going to cut everybody's throat." He pulled up the long curved knife that he was holding in his hand and shook it menacingly.

"Son, we don't have much cash or jewellery." Dadu calmly said. "The old women have a few ounce of gold and I have couple of hundred taka in cash. If that's what you are looking for I'll get you that."

Before he could finish dadi came out of the house holding a small packet in his hand. "Here's all my jewellery. Please take. Dear, give them the two hundred taka. Don't make them mad."

The leader of the dacoits impatiently looked at the rest of his group. Clearly he was very annoyed. One of his team members who were standing at the back suddenly said," Army's wife is here."

The voice was slightly muffled as it came from below the thin towel but it surely sounded familiar.

"That sounded like Mintu." Jhima whispered in my ears. "He worked here as a day labourer, helped in harvesting the grains. That bastard brought these dacoits!"

I had seen Mintu bhai a few times. He was a little shy type, in his early twenties. It was hard for me to understand why in the whole world he would bring these dacoits in our house. At the same time I wasn't sure who he was referring to as 'Army's wife'.

Dadu and dadi looked quite worried now. "She is eight months pregnant." Dadi pleaded. "She has a few more ounces of gold ornaments. If that's what you are looking for I'll go get them. Please wait here. I'll be back in no time..."

The leader looked suspicious. "No, you wait here oldie. Let me go check."

Dadu took a stand this time. "Watch it! If you touch her..."

The leader grabbed dadu by the neck. "What are you going to do old man? I can kill you anytime. Guys, keep an eye on them. If anybody makes a noise just cut the throat."

He started to climb up the stairs toward my grandparent's bedroom. This is when I suddenly real-ized what was happening. They were talking about my mother! I felt this sudden rush of anger in me. Jhima was holding me tightly. I shook her hands off me, unbolted the door and jumped outside the hut. "Don't touch my mother." I shouted with every bit of strength that I had. "When I grow up I'll kill all of you.

MIntu bhai, I'll tell the police that you brought the dacoits."

For a second the yard turned completely silent. The leader standing half way up the stairs watched me with shear amazement. Then he roared, "You bastard Mintu, even this little kid recognized you. Finish him off."

Jhima had walked out and stood by me. Fearing for my life she lit up like a fire. Her thunderous voice echoed in the darkness of the village. "If you touch him I swear upon god every member of your families will die in leprosy. Your kids will die in fever. Your houses will burn into ashes. Your grains will be eaten by the rats..."

Suddenly we heard a lot of noise outside the boundary walls. There were more shouts and footsteps at a distance approaching fast. It was clear that the villagers had found out that the dacoits had attacked my grandparent's house and they had come to help.

"Let's get out of here, boss." One of the members of the dacoits fearfully said. "If we get caught they'll beat us to death."

The leader looked scared as well. No matter how dreadful they were they had no chance against hundreds of villagers who would mercilessly kill them if gotten an opportunity. He ran down the stairs.

"We have to get out through the back door. Mintu, where is the back door?"

Mintu ran toward the back of the house. The rest followed him. In the next few seconds they were out in the garden. We could hear their footsteps quickly moving away. The villagers started to bang on the front door. Dadu opened it up.

Shahid chacha was standing at the front of the crowd holding a long bamboo stick. His wife stood right by him with a special vegetable cutter (boti). Alek Mia stood behind them with a sharp spear in his hand. They were accompanied by at least fifteen to twenty men and women. All of them made a living working in this household. During the time of need they had rushed in to help before anybody else did. Dadu hugged Shahid chacha tightly. "The bastards ran away." His voice almost closed in tears. "You guys came at the right time."

"Don't worry, Morol sahib." Shahid chacha said. "We'll guard the house for the rest of the night."

Within a few minutes another thirty to forty people with sticks from the neighbouring houses rushed in to help. There were several young men in this group. They dared to chase the dacoits through the garden. Uncle Shahid and the others spent the rest of the night in the courtyard. Jhima held me tightly in her lap, closed the door and lied down on the bed. I checked on mom as soon as I had a chance. She was very nervous, her face white in fear. Dadi sat by her and tried to comfort her. "I'm heading for

Khulna tomorrow." Mom tearfully repeated. "I can't stay here for another night."

Next day dadu arranged for us to make the trip to Khulna. He decided to accompany us as well. Around noon we packed up all our stuff and started. As usual Alek was going to take us to Kaligonj. He handed over his cattle to another boy for the day. Jhima hugged me dearly and cried her heart off. "Will I see you again, Khoka? When will you come again? Will I still be alive?"

All the tears made me somewhat tearful as well. I muttered something under my breath before running to catch up with the bullock cart that already started its slow journey. Looking back I saw jhima, dadi along with several other villagers standing quietly. Suddenly I felt an overwhelming surge of emotions. They all seemed so much of an integral part of my existence. A mixed sense of loss and agony flooded me. The house, the yards, the orchards with all its exciting varieties of fruit trees, the bamboo groves, and the ponds - everything seemed so precious and endearing! With my vision blurried as tear filled my eyes I quietly climbed up on grandpa's bike. We rode slowly beside the bullock cart on the meandering dirt road, behind remained a plethora of my most cherished memories.

Chapter 11

Once we reached Khulna mom collapsed on khala's lap and cried profusely. We moved into the same room where we stayed before. There was no news of Roni bhai yet but everybody believed he was in India. Once his training was completed he would return with other fighters. I was really surprised to see how Moni bhai had changed in just a few days. He had almost totally stopped gathering with his friends at the den and spent most of his time alone. When I went to see him in the den he gestured me to sit down. "It's good that you folks returned here."

I nodded. "After the robbery mom got very scared."

Moni bhai lit a cigarette and silently smoked for a little while. "What do you think? Is Bangladesh good or Pakistan?"

I didn't have to think too much. "Bangladesh is better. Our struggle is for freedom."

Moni bhai let go a heavy sigh. "You are just a boy, you wouldn't understand this. Once Bangladesh is born the Hindus will rule this country. Today they serve in our houses. Then they will turn us into their servants. Do you know how the Muslims live in India?"

He paced up and down restlessly. "Roni joined the war. He is better off. I can't concentrate on anything. What is more important – religion or country? Pakistan or India..."

"You mean Bangladesh?"

"Bangladesh? My foot. It's going to be India. We'll be nothing by suckers of India. Today Pakis are robbing us, next the Indians will."

"Do you want to go to the war, Moni bhai? If I was older I would have definitely gone. They killed so many people the other day. I would shoot them all dead."

"Be thankful that you are just a kid. Be truly thankful. Why should I go to the war? My mind doesn't approve it. Let it go. Do you want to eat singara?"

They were fried delicious treats, made of flour dough and spicy vegetable or meat filler. I nodded thankfully. It was one of my favourite foods. We walked to the small stall of Kumar and occupied the broken wooden bench that was placed in front of his stall. Kumar was famous for his singara. He never let Moni bhai pay. Slowly in the next hour or so several of Moni bhai's friends gathered there. Any other time they would all get into noisy discussions but today I found them quiet, unmindful. I went back home. Mom was feeling bad again. She liked it when I stayed near her.

In the evening the house seemed empty. Mom was lying on the bed in her room. Khala was with her. They chatted in low voice. Rushi went to the floor right above to play with the little girl of the family that rented it. Parvoti's mom was handling the kitchen. Usually khala cooked, Parvoti's mom helped. I peeked into mom's room on my way to the veranda. The empty cage of the parrot was still hanging. That made me even sadder. Yunus had left. Nobody knew where he went. Khala believed he had also joined Roni bhai for the training. Khalu thought he didn't have the guts to go in a war. Possibly he found a better paying job somewhere else. Didn't look like his absence caused any difficulties in this household. He hardly helped in any housework anyway. In addition he was frequently getting into arguments with Moni bhai who gave him a smack on the face one day. He left after that. I learned this from khala.

I could hear khalu talking excitedly from his chamber. The door was closed so I couldn't see his visitors. But I knew like most of his party members he was a supporter of Pakistani government. He had no interest in joining hands with Hindu inhabited India to become separate from Muslim Pakistan. But he didn't believe in killings. Even though he had hatred for Hindu majority India nobody could suggest that he had any hatred for the people from Hindu community. Instead his friendly nature had made him quite popular among both Hindus and Muslims in the community. He had organized a peace committee to ensure that people in the neighbourhood remained calm and peaceful. Nevertheless, one thing I had noticed with amazement that whenever he mentioned Roni bhai he could barely hid his pride. He might have not supported this particular war but he was proud of the fact that one of his sons had the courage to stick to his ideology and fight a cause that he believed to be right. Moni bhai must have noticed it as well because he had stopped joining the family for supper. He ate later, alone.

Little after midnight mom's water broke. Rushi and I were sleeping. We both woke up in mom's painful scream. Khala came running.

"What's happening, Jaira?"

"I think it's time, bubu (sister)," Mom said, "Sermon the midwife."

The only midwife who served the area was Turzo's mom. She was Parvoti's neighbour. Khala ran to the veranda at the back and called out for her. "O Turzo's mom! Turzo's mom! Jaira's water broke!"

Turzo's mom and Parvoti's mom both stepped out of their huts. Within ten minutes they gathered few other women and came into the house. In the mean time Rushi and I got driven out of mom's room. The lady on the next floor took Rushi with her. She would sleep with her little daughter for the night. Moni bhai climbed down hearing all the noise. I stayed with him. Just in case there was a need I wouldn't have to go looking for him. Only Turzo's mom and khala were allowed to enter into mom's room while the rest of the women started a lively chat on the corridor. Khalu paced restlessly in his room. "Why don't we take her in a hospital?" He questioned khala every time she walked in. "This is a serious matter."

Khala chided him. "Both your boys were born in the hand of Turzo's mother. Why are you suddenly making such a big fuss about hospitals? Jaira is doing perfectly fine. The baby is placed properly. There will be no difficulties in birth. Why don't you go back to bed and try to get some sleep?"

"Are you nuts? How can I sleep in a situation like this?"

Khalu continued with his pacing. Moni bhai and I sat on the tiny porch in front of mom's room. I didn't even know when I fell asleep propping against Moni bhai. The cry of a newly born baby woke me up. Moni bhai must have fallen asleep too. He rubbed his eyes with the back of his hands. "You have a new brother. Go, see him."

I sprung into my feet and bolted in mom's room. There was this tiny baby lying right by mom. I checked it out with amazement. It cried louder at my sight. Mom weakly said," Looks exactly like you, only the hair is curly."

I hugged mom. "I am going to love him a lot. I'll never hurt him. I promise."

Rest of the night passed by quickly. In the morning the neighbouring women came along their children to see the baby. It felt like a big festival. Khalu bought plenty of sweets and had them distributed among the neighbours. I ate to my heart's content.

About a week later after lot of pondering the baby was named Milky. I can't remember who had first proposed the name but it must have had something to do with his frequent feeding tendency. Pretty soon we became quite close. He would twist his lips at my sight. The only sad thing was that for some strange reason he liked Rushi more than me. He went ballistic with his hands and legs as soon as she went near him. I couldn't understand why would he like a girl so much, especially someone who nagged all the time.

Few weeks elapsed since Milky was born. One evening we ate our supper, played a little bit before being sent to bed. Rushi and I slept next to mom. Milky slept in one side and us on the other. Not sure how late it was but we all woke up in a big commotion. For a little while I could only hear a lot of noise but nothing meaningful. Slowly as my head cleared up I started to understand what it was all about. A few young men were calling out khalu by his name. There iron gate in the entrance of the house was followed by a small yard and then a long porch. All the bedrooms were along this porch, ours first, then khalu's and a third one sometimes used as a guest room. The young men were standing on the porch. I could hear the sound of glass panels breaking, must be of the windows.

"Come out, Mosabber. Come out you bastard. You are an accomplice of the Pakistanis. Today is the end of line for you. Come out you murderer." Several voices roared.

Mom held two of us tightly and trembled in morbid fear. Milky had woken up in all these noise and was howling at the top of his voice. At this point we heard the bolt in khalu's room making a cracking noise and the door opening. Next we heard khalu's voice. "Who are you calling murderer? Me? Who did I murder? When? Answer me. I am a true Muslim. I'll never hold hands with the Hindus. Is that my sin? Is that why you rascals want to kill me?"

His words were sunk by the trembling voice of khala, "Sons, don't you all know him very well? He doesn't harm anybody. You guys are freedom fighters. Why would you kill a good man? My one son went to war. You know Roni, don't you? He went to the war."

"Your husband is a Pakistani spy." One young man yelled back at khala. "We want independent Bangladesh. We want to kick those bastard murderers out of this land. Your husband held hand with those murderers. We want eye for an eye. Go on, kill that spy." He gestured at another young man with a gun.

Khala shrieked.

"Go ahead, shoot me." Khalu sounded all pumped up. "I don't fear death. I have followed the words of Allah all my life. Shoot..."

Suddenly mom released us and jumped off the bed, her fear gone. Possessed in a burst of braveness and strength she unbolted the door and rushed out to the porch. I ran after her. Rushi hid under the bed and joined Milky in a crying contest.

Once out in the porch I was horrified to notice that two young men had really advanced at khalu with their rifles levelled at his heart. Several other youth with guns stood on the porch. To everybody's bewilderment mom ran in front of the two advancing young men and stood with her hands extended as a blockade. "Don't do this, boys. I am not saying this because he is my brother-in-law but I have never seen him harming anybody. All Hindus in the neighbourhood comes here when in trouble. They trust him with their lives. Please don't hurt him."

"Move out of our way, apa (sis). If we don't shed blood as a response to the murders they committed, those bastard Pakistanis won't stop. They have made this country a killing field. Cohorts like this man are allowing them to continue in their barbarian invasion. We need to kill them all one by one."

"Shoot." Khalu boldly repeated his open invitation. "I am not afraid of you. I only fear Allah. Shoot me."

Mom held the hands of the young men and begged, "All of you are sons of Khulna. Most of you know this man more or less. Have any of you ever heard him hurting anybody? Have mercy, let him live. Please don't do this."

The youths turned soft in her pleadings. They exchanged glances. Mom continued," Go on, boys. I'll pray for you. Free Bangladesh from the enemies. We are all so proud of you."

The youths looked restless as they glanced around. Situation wasn't very safe. Pakistani soldiers might show up getting tips from the neighbourhood. Before leaving they cautioned khalu," If you ever harm any freedom fighter we won't spare your life next time."

"My son went in the war." Khalu raised a fist in the air and proudly said. "I would never harm any of you, remember that. I am a true Muslim not a killer. I'll embrace death without fear when my time comes."

Before leaving the youths did something unexpected. They touched my mom's feet asking for her blessings. "Apa, please pray that we can free this country and come back alive to our families."

Mom could no longer stop her tears. "I am always praying, boys. Every time I sit on the prayer mat, I pray for each and every one of you. Be care-ful..."

The team of the freedom fighters disap-peared quickly in the darkness. With them gone eve-rything abruptly turned unusually silent for a few moments. Mom collapsed on the stairs, tired and shaken she burst into silent tears with her face drowned between her knees. Khala and khalu almost picked her up and put her back on the bed. At this point Moni bhai came down tip toed. Finding me cu-riously observing him he explained," I know those boys. They are juniors to me. They would have in-sulted me if I came down. It was good thing that Roni went to the war. You must pick a side. Staying in the middle is no good. You get harassed by both parties."

We shut down all the doors and windows of the house and spent the rest of the night awake. Mom fell asleep around the morning. Khala tried her best but could not take khalu back to the bed. He continued to pace briskly up and down the corridor.

Chapter 12

Finally, after plenty of effort, dad got a family quarter around the first week of August in Chaman, Baluchistan. The few Bengali doctors who worked in Pakistan continued to perform their job quietly. The impact of the war wasn't that apparent yet. The news media in the West Pakistan took every attempt to describe it as lightly and incorrectly as possible. They portrayed it as a conspiracy of India and Awami league. For the Bengali officers and soldiers posted in East Pakistan choosing a side was an easy decision to make. However, personnel who were posted in West Pakistan lived in fear and confusion. They had no way to leave and risked serious consequences if attempted. In a situation like this their primary goal was to move their families to safety.

Once the house became available dad arranged for us to make the trip. Coincidentally we boarded the last PIA flight from Dhaka to Karachi in mid August right before all flights got suspended due to the war. Four of us – mom, Rushi, I and Milky in mom's lap with his eyes bulging out in utter amazement, left Bangladesh for a land totally unknown.

Khalu had come to Dhaka with us. We stayed with a distant uncle for two days. He saw us off in the airport and waited until we were airborne. Khala wanted to come as well but she had to stay back to take care of the family. Before boarding the plane mom embraced khalu and wept quietly. She had grown up in this family as a child since her mother died. To mom khala and khalu were much more than just sister and brother-in-law. Khalu wiped off his eyes under his glasses.

The flight to Karachi took much longer than usual as we had to fly via Ceylon. We didn't have permission to fly over India. The most frustrating part of the flight was Milky's non-stopped howling and Rushi's continuous nagging. Most troubling moments were during take off and landing as our ears got plugged. They were too young and cried not know-ing what was happening. Frustrated, Mom was quite mad with dad. Why couldn't he come to Dhaka and accompany us in this trip? Even I knew it wasn't pos-sible. When mad her rationality diminished, I figured. Fortunately, dad was able to take a week off from work and came to Karachi to receive us. Rushi and I jumped into his lap as he waited for us in Karachi air-port. He smiled victoriously.

"How have you been, kids?'

"Do you have any common sense?" mom snapped, before we had a chance to respond. "Did you ever think what I may have to go through travel-ling with these three monkeys?"

Dad smiled ear to ear and picked Milky up in his lap. Milky gave out a huge cry. "Dad! Dad!" We tried to explain to him. "Why are you crying?"

He wasn't about to listen to us. Once re-turned to mom's lap he stopped crying and watched dad with his big baby eyes.

"Even if I wanted to I couldn't have gone back to Dhaka." Dad explained. "Government isn't allow-ing anybody to return now. Be grateful that you were able to come. This was the last flight."

Mom continued to grumble, still quite agi-tated. Ayesha apa and Jaman bhai had come to the airport to receive us as well. Jaman bhai worked in a government organization. They had been living in Karachi for long. Ayesha apa, a distant cousin sister of ours, was known to be rude and bipolar. However, she looked happy at our sight, to my relief. We col-lected our luggage and made our way out of the air-port. The first thing that caught my eyes was the crowd. People crammed the streets in unbelievable numbers. Most part of my life I had either spent in villages or small towns. I was quite taken by the crowd and the assortment of vendors. Rushi who usually remained engaged with her useless dolls was also equally surprised. Only Milky didn't know the difference and cried his head off.

Jaman bhai and Ayesha Apa lived in a small place but yet they had graciously welcomed us to stay with them for a few days. Dad didn't yet have a chance to see Karachi at all. This was an attractive city and tourists flocked here from all over the world. It would be a mistake if we didn't take this opportu-nity to check the city out.

We stayed in Karachi for four days and visited numerous attractions, of which a couple stuck in my mind quite strongly - visit to the Clifton beach and the grave of Quaid-e-Azam.

Clifton beach, situated by Arabian Sea was not too far from the city. The beautiful sand extended far away. There was an aquarium and a facility to ride camel and horses. This was a place where many city dwellers came to escape from the crowded Karachi to get some fresh air and relax in the soft sand.

This was my first visit to a sea beach. I was speechless at the beauty of the surroundings – the long sandy beach looked the most beautiful thing in the world as the blue waves of Arabian Sea constantly broke against it and slowly but softly touched my bare feet with its cool, pleasing touch. I had earlier followed the steps of dad and hung my showes on my shoulder after tying them together with shoestrings. Mom stayed out of the reach of the waves with Milky. I walked over the sand along the shore line with my feet making clear prints on the soft sand. Rushi followed me from a safe distance. I waved at her to join me but she didn't come. Mom was calling me back. I unwillingly returned. There was no good in agitating her. I also wanted to check out the Aquarium.

The aquarium was located in a building close to the beach. It consisted of several large tanks of different sizes housing many varieties of saltwater fishes and giant turtles. This was an amazing experience for all of us. This was mom's first as well and she showed equal excitement as the kids. Milky who never did anything but cry had also remained calm and watched the strange animals. I was quite taken by the sharks in display. I had read so many stories about them. They had razor sharp teeth and could neatly cut off limbs from a human body. As they swam in circles with their slick bodies I watched them in pure awe and possibly some apprehension. Later dad had to pull me away from there.

Next we went to ride the camels and horses. Mom had a long time desire to ride a horse. She had read stories about Rajia Sultana since a kid, the Indian princess who fought battles riding a horse along with male soldiers. The desire sort of grew up from there. I heard in old days there were many horses in the villages. During his youth even nana had horses too. Once he became a family man and had kids he had gotten rid of that expensive hobby.

Mom passed on Milky to dad's lap and went to ride a horse. After quite a bit of struggle she finally made it on the horse's back but as soon as the animal started to move her face turned white as a paper. "I am going to fall! I am going to fall!" She screamed in panic.

The Urdu speaking horse owner tried to calm her down with his comforting smile and soft words but that didn't do any good. She continued to scream, begging to be relieved from this predicament. Even Rushi burst into giggle. Once taken down mom was so relieved that she sat right on the sand. We all laughed at her a bit. Little Milky joined us too without knowing what was all the fuss about.

I was more interested in climbing on a camel. I expressed that to dad who took me to the camel owner. He had the camel sit on the ground and helped me on its back. As it slowly stood up I totally jammed. From the ground it didn't seem like the animal was that tall. Falling from its back was definitely going to be pretty painful. I held on to the saddle hard. The camel walked slowly. With every step it took its back moved heavily, making me think that I was about to slip down. Overall a thrilling experience. After getting down I labored to look normal though inside I was quite relieved. Any display of weakness would allow mom and Rushi to tease me. Dad climbed both the horse and the camel. No amount of pleading worked with Rushi. She had no interest in riding anything that was living. She stayed with mom, holding one end of her saree.

The grave of Quaid-e-Azam was quite amazing as well. Everything was so neat and glazing. Quaid-e-Azam Mohammed Ali Jinnah was the founder of Pakistan. After Second World War the British emperor decided to free India. During that tumultuous time he worked with Gandhi to create a separate nation for the Muslims apart from India. West and East Pakistan were the regions where most Muslims lived, hence these two parts constituted one Pakistan. I read some in the book, heard the rest from dad. Currently the war that broke down was between East and West Pakistan. Dad had already explained to me why East Pakistan was trying to separate. The central government of Pakistan had been acting as an authoritarian entity toward the East part since the very beginning. He made no reservation expressing to me his desire to leave Pakistan but unfortunately he was helpless for the time being.

We were to make the journey to Quetta from Karachi on a train. It was supposed to be a day long trip. From there we would be heading for Chaman - another seven eight hours train trip. Our plan was to stay overnight in Quetta. Dad had a few acquaintances in the Quetta cantonment who he wanted to meet. We would get some rest as well.

Our train started one beautiful sunny morning. When I was a little kid I had ridden in trains but I could barely remember. After arriving in the train station just watching this long snake like giant machine with huge lined compartments and big steel wheels Rushi and I both were quite astounded. We gave our constant bickerings a break and joined forces to count the compartments. We couldn't finish counting them all as dad called us back when he noticed we were drifting too far away from them. Milky seemed to be very keen to share our joy as well. He threw his hands and legs in the air and struggled with mom to slip down from her lap onto the platform.

The train departed little later. We received tickets for first class and were very happy getting our own little room, especially mom. She had to feed Milky and didn't feel comfortable doing it in public. Ignoring repeated request from our parents Rushi and I stuck our heads out of the windows as far as we could and watched the long train wiggle forward like a serpent. There was nothing compared to the beauty of that view. And the constant sound of the wheels rolling and the whistles blowing ... chuga chuga chuga chuga choo choo ..., it felt like we were heading toward a land of dreams riding on a mythical animal. Our excitement must have annoyed mom because she bitterly said, ``Why are you kids so happy? Who knows which cave are we heading to?"

The word cave increased our excitement even further. If we were really going to live in a cave that wouldn't be too bad at all! Hope of something so bizarre happening disappeared soon. Dad chuckled. "Just because we are going in a rocky region doesn't mean we'll be living in caves."

"We'll see about that." Mom shot back. "I heard only mountain people lives there and it's very cold. How am I going to live there alone with this little baby?"

"We'll be living inside the cantonment." Dad comforted. "On the other hand people are not bad. They are actually very friendly."

Mom didn't look happy. In the mean time dad sat with us to answer our questions, especially mine. Where was Quetta? Where was Chaman? What was there? Who lived there? Etc. Pretty soon I learned quite a bit about the region we were heading to.

Quetta was the capital of the province named Baluchistan. The town was located in the proximity of Afghanistan, Iran and Pakistan borders close to the impenetrable Bolan Pass. 5500 feet above the sea level it was surrounded by mountains. Each of these mountains had beautiful names – Chiltan, Takatu, Mordar, Jarghun. Due to its location it became the most significant military base in whole Pakistan. It was about five hundred fifty miles away from Karachi, about seven hundred and fifty miles from Lahore and about a thousand miles from Peshawar. The name Quetta came from the Pashtu word 'quetta' which meant castle. In reality due to its mountainous location it did enjoy a castle like advantage. During eleventh century after king Mahmud of Gazhni occupied Quetta its reputation increased by manifold. In the year 1543 Mogul Emperor Humayun stopped here to rest on his way back from Persia. When he left he arranged for his one year old son Akbar to stay here. Akbar lived here for the next couple of years. Humayun later came back to take him back with him. Moguls ruled Quetta until 1556. After that it was conquered by the Persians. Later in 1595 Akbar conquered it back from them.

In 1839 during Afghan war the town tempo-rarily went under the rule of the British who suc-ceeded in strengthening their foothold here. After the division of India the population here increased drastically mainly because of military base and the massive commercialized cultivation projects. Unfor-tunately on 31st May 1935 the populous town was almost totally destroyed owing to a devastating earthquake. Forty thousand people had met their ends. From that land of dead the town slowly rose back again. But this time the town was built much simplistically keeping in mind the future possibility of more earthquakes.

I didn't know when I had fallen asleep listen-ing to dad. When I woke up I found the train stopped in a station. All of us climbed down on the platform. As I ran along the train Rushi rushed to join me. This was something new. Most times I couldn't get her do things with me, not even by pleading. We ran all the way to the end. Dad and mom allowed us as there were only a handful of people in the station and we were never out of their sight. We ran our way back as well. Rushi was gasping for air midway. I helped her back. It was a pleasure to see that finally she was starting to see how much fun there was beyond her stupid, cute looking dolls. I could not tolerate those dolls. Though mom always mentioned that as a little boy I frequently played with dolls when in the com-pany of Rani apa. What a bloody shame!

The train departed again. Clickity clack, clickity clack ... the usual melody followed us along the way. Rushi went back to sleep tiredly. Milky was observing me with his big eyes. I smiled at him. "When we grow up we'll become good friends, remember that." I thought. He seemed to know what I was thinking because he smiled back. At that moment we two brothers built a bridge that would never break in our lifetime. Nobody else noticed what had just happened. Dad was reading, mom trying to sleep. I looked out through the window. The heat of the sun was decreasing slowly. The soft rays of the afternoon sun flooded the nature with affection. Slowly the pattern of the land was changing as well. There were fewer and fewer trees, more barren, and dry land. Dad mentioned that Baluchistan was desert like, mountainous; not like the province Sindh which was green with abundance of plants. Karachi was in Sindh. All my life I had spent in the naturally beautiful Bangladesh where the sky was deep blue and the ground was amazingly green. The love and affection that I had for greeneries would never go away but deep inside me I also felt this mysterious call of the desert, the mountains. The rough and the mystic land waved at me as if to say, "Come Khoka, come." I stuck my head out of the window. Where are you? How far? When would I see you? The long train ran faster and faster as it buzzed into my ears, "Almost there, almost there." As more and more hills popped up in the views I eagerly tried to look beyond them, my whole body shivered in the anticipation of the ensuing new world. How far are you?

The closer we got to Quetta the landscape continually turned more and more rugged. Our train rolled up scaling the steep slopes of stony mountains. Additional engine was attached to strengthen its power needed for the journey uphill. The sound of its rhythmic movement echoed in the ridges ... Clickity clack, clickity clack. Clickity clack, clickity clack. I listened to that sound with all my heart. It felt as if we were going in this impossible mission through the beautiful but dangerous land around us. The further we went the denser the mystery turned. The best parts were the tunnels. As the train passed through assortment of tunnels, small to big, everything turned completely dark. Suddenly the sound of the wheels increased manifold, almost hurting the ears. The pitch black darkness along with the loud reverberating echoes made me shivering in excitement. My hair stood up in anticipation every time we approached a tunnel. Rushi must have felt the same way because she held my hand tightly as we peeked through the window into the darkness. Moments after we passed through it the darkness would blend into the shining sun, blinding us with flash of brightness.

"What are you kids watching?" Mom inquired, finding us glued to the window.

Rushi was three but had a pathetic vocabulary. "Mountains. Big mountains." The answer miraculously came from her.

"What's so interesting about mountains? They all look same." Mom muttered.

I didn't try to explain this to her. She had no heart for all these natural stuff – mountains, rivers, creeks. All she did was to drive us to either eat or sleep and be bossy all the time. Dad was sleeping on a bunker. He had gone through this route a few times. His interest in nature wasn't too bad but repeat trips could take away the thrill – I concluded. "Tullen, tullen." Rushi added as if to answer mom. She still had issues with 'l' and 'n'. My attempts to correct her usually met with frantic objections and denials hence I stopped trying. Someday she would definitely figure it out, I hoped.

I didn't realize when I fell asleep. At the first light of the morning I jumped out of my bed. The deep red sun rising at the backdrop of the blue sky and the riffs was a mind blowing view. This was my first trip to the mountains. Mesmerized I observed how a new day embraced this rough, rocky land with the rays glittering between the occasional tree leaves and meandering thin streams. I watched with all my heart and listened with all my soul as the train continued in its journey – rugged land, barren desert, rugged land, barren desert..."

Thanks to dad I was already familiar with Nazrul's work, one of the most prolific writers of Bengali language. In these unique surroundings snippets of his writings came to me naturally.

Rugged land, barren desert, a distance hard to pass,

Conquer we must, sailing in dark after night-fall,

Watch out partners!

...What could be more thrilling and interesting than this journey?

After twenty four hours in the train we finally reached Quetta. Here we were to stay a day in one of dad's friend's house. Then we would start for Chaman, another seven-eight hours of train. Chaman was located almost next to the border with Afghanistan. We would be going through the famous Khojak Pass. I really didn't want to get down from the train in Quetta. Anyway, that night we stayed in the house of Captain Bajlur. His wife Saleha was very nice. They cordially welcomed us in their house and treated us very well. Their only son Moti quickly became my friend. He was about the same age of me and we played together for long time mostly running around in the house. Rushi also joined us. Usually I would have discouraged her but in the train we had made some sort of connection. She had proven to me that she could go beyond her stupid dolls if she wanted to.

In the afternoon we went to the bazaar situated on Jinnah road. The place was crowded with

Pathans wearing their usual head dressing (pagri) and the Beluchi hawkers wearing hand designed red hats. The local mountain women covered in colourful dresses were selling cloths with flashy designs and sequence work.   There wasn't a thing that one wouldn't find there. From handicrafts to far coats, shoes and sandals, Afghani carpets, colourful decorative stones, all kind of fruits, nuts, pistachio etc. We purchased some food. Rushi wanted to buy a small shawl made for kids. Dad didn't have much money left and had to pass. At her tender age how would Rushi know all the complexity about money? She shed some tears in protest. I liked a pair of mountain shoes but didn't even have the courage to bring it up to dad's attention.

Later at night the adults chatted until very late. After the long train trip Milky must have been very tired because he slept like a rock which gave mom some time to relax. Rushi was still sad for that shawl and cried to sleep. Moti and I played mock shooting games for a while. After we broke a water glass the parents interrupted and forced us to bed.

Next morning we got into another train. I felt a little sad saying good bye to Moti. Coming so far from the familiar land and making a friend in such a short notice wasn't a regular thing. I invited him to visit us in Chaman before climbing up into our compartment. Captain Bajlur and Saleha repeatedly mentioned that they would definitely visit us at the first chance they got. Little later our train moved ahead leaving the three of them behind on the station.

Rugged land, barren desert.... Clickity clack... Rugged land, barren desert....The feeling of shivering returned. Such wonderful feeling I felt only when I walked on the dusty roads of my village. Memories of dadu, dadi, jhima, Rani Apa, Minu Apa and many others flashed before my eyes. I wondered how they were all doing. The war was going on in full force, people were dying. I heard Captain Bajlur and dad discussing about it gravely. They had to be very careful. Even a slight suspicion of treason could be the cause of court martial. There was no chance for any of them to join the independence war of Bangladesh from here. There only option was to wait for the right moment. Low ranked officers and ordinary soldiers were yet to show any disrespect to them but there was no telling that the situation won't change. Nobody wanted to put their families into a dire situation. In public they restrained from showing any interest about the ongoing war. There was no reason to make anybody suspicious.

The train continued its journey through the elevations. I heard that the trip to Chaman was even more thrilling than to Quetta. The reason was not difficult to see. This was a totally mountainous terrain with tall peaks and ridges as it approached the Afghanistan border. Kandahar wasn't too far from here. The biggest attraction and the most thrilling part of this train trip was the Khojak Pass tunnel. Located about 7500 feet above the ground this tunnel was 3.2 miles long and ended in the Pakistan Railway Terminal in Chaman. Dad mentioned that it was the longest tunnel in South Asia, a wonderful specimen of engineering marvel. The work had started around the end of eighteen century. The tunnel was dug simultaneously from two end of the mountain body and was supposed to meet half way down. However in reality things didn't go as planned and story went that the engineer who was in charge tried to commit suicide. Later a solution was found and the tunnel was opened for use in 1892.

Rushi and I eagerly waited for the Khojak Pass tunnel. We had been going through numerous small tunnels but after hearing about the giant nothing else impressed us anymore. In his attempt to keep us occupied dad started to talk about the rock formations that surrounded us. Thousands of years ago as a result of frequent earthquakes and volcanic eruptions various types of rocks were created in this part of Baluchistan. There were two main lava stream in this region – uh-uh and pa-hoy-hoy. The stones that looked like twisted ropes or the triangular boulders were all created from lava. Often they looked as if some artist unmindfully created such beautiful sculptures. Uh-uh and Pa-hoy-hoy the two words were originated from Hawaiian. The stream of lava that contained triangular pieces is called uh-uh. Such lava streams could be as thick as 100 meters. On the other hand Pa-hoy-hoy flowed smoothly and was only a meter thick. Beside the lava rocks this region had its own look and feel, something one can only find here.

Finally we entered the Khojak pass tunnel. Like a mythical monster from the magical world of imagination our vehicle slithered its way into the dark world. Suddenly we discovered ourselves in a mysterious world submerged into the eternal darkness. The monster's angry roars echoed again and again on to the walls of the cave until they slowly died off and new stronger echoes took their places. I was completely lost in this strange world of darkness, roars and echoes. I stood with my eyes wide open, ears standing. Rushi stood by me holding the bottom of my shorts tightly. Mom was awake. She impatiently said," How long is this thing? When is it going to end?"

Mom was afraid of darkness, especially if she was in tight space. Milky slept in peace. He didn't even know what he missed. May be on our way back he would be old enough to understand. Who knew when we could return?

The train moved slowly. Time seemed to stop in the underground world. "Watch out! Watch out! Watch out!" The monster made its way through the darkness cautiously. Finally a flash of light popped up at the end of the tunnel hinting the end of it. I let go a deep breath, slowly, little sad. Mom was relieved. "Finally! I can't stand tunnels."

Slowly we emerged out into the sun, leaving behind the mystic world.

Chaman.

Small town but the cantonment was comparatively large. Dad was able to secure an officer's quarter - specious two bedroom house. Mom liked it instantly. There weren't too many officers in this location. In total six-seven with two families from Bangladesh – Major Altaf and Major Jafor. Both of them were senior to dad but they became good friends. Dad was the first doctor here. Aunt Nuri, Major Altaf's wife, was very social person. She arrived with plenty of cooked food the first day we moved in there. With her came their two children – Roushan bhai and Rushni apa. They couldn't have been older than 14 and 12 respectively. Both were easygoing, cheerful. They were very happy to have Rushi and me. Clearly they weren't having much of a good time in Chaman. They had no friends in here. There was no school either. As a result whenever new kids came in they became excited. We liked both of them very much too. They lived just couple of house apart.

Major Jafor and his wife Aunt Asifa were on the quieter side. They had two sons – Bashar and Ratul. Bashar was a year older than me, Ratul was a year younger. It didn't take us too long to get going. However, I soon realized that Aunt Nuri and Aunt Asifa were not in best of terms and the two families had limited social connections. After we moved in mom invited both the families several times. We also joined them for dinners and other functions. It took considerable effort but eventually the ice broke.

Chaman was located right next to Afghanistan border. In this region beside Beluchis presence of Pastuns were very prominent. They were very religious and independent minded. Women didn't wear traditional burkha but wore all covering colourful clothes revealing their faces only. Men wore traditional loose pyjama, long kurta and either Pagri or hat on their heads. Most of them were pretty big. The first local family that we got to know was Jahir Khan and his family.

Jahir was Beluchi. He was very poor and worked as a gardener in the cantonment. Even though civilians weren't supposed to live inside the cantonment an exception was made for him. The officers had arranged for him to stay inside the cantonment near the officer's quarters. It was an old brick building where Jahir lived with his wife Fatima, mother and half crazy brother Amir Khan. He was mild in manners and shy with words. He worked quietly. Their house couldn't have been more than a quarter of a mile away from where we lived. Bashar, Ratul and I went down there quite frequently. Fatima had no children. She seemed pretty young. She liked us very much. To earn some extra money she used to work with her mother-in-law, sewing cloths in colourful designs with sequences and selling them. Many of the officer's wives bought those. Some they sold in the market. At our sight she always smiled affectionately.

"How are you boys today?" would be the first thing she said.

Next she would quickly bring out some loz-enges from a glass container and distribute among us. Cheap stuff but tasted delicious. Three of us fought for those. However, beside Fatima we had another reason to visit Jahir's house. It was Amir Khan. Right in the middle of the front yard of the house Amir was digging a deep hole. He used to spend most of his time during day digging. It was close to 10 feet deep and going deeper. Untrimmed beard and layered in dirt Amir continued to work with his shovel hours after hour. We stood by the hole and watched him with deadly curiosity. He never really cared about our presence. Still Fatima would always caution us, "Not a word. When mad he can be dangerous."

After such warning we would take a step back. We wondered how he might have lost his mind in such young age. Jahir's mother was old but very nice. Like Fatima she enjoyed our presence as well. Sometimes she would even tell us stories. We learned from her that since his childhood Amir had been suffering from an untreatable disease. There was no good physician in the area. Even if there was they probably wouldn't be able to afford his service. She was very much worried about Amir. A few years back when her husband died he had instructed Jahir to look after his brother. It was a big burden on Jahir but yet he did his best. He even took him to local doctors who practiced traditional medicine a few times but they couldn't provide any treatment. The old woman wanted to get him married but wondered where would she find a girl who would agree to marry her crazy son.

It could get pretty cold in Chaman, especially in December, we learned. At the end of August the weather was comfortable, especially for the kids. We ran all around the cantonment area. Sometimes we even allowed Rushi to join us. One day she did something very unusual. She went for a mid afternoon stroll or something like that on her own. When mom started to panic not finding her anywhere she could think off I was alarmed as well. Bashar, Ratul and I joined mom to look for Rushi, even dad came back from work. Finally we found her in Jahir's house. It was Fatima who waved me in. Stepping inside I saw Rushi sitting comfortably on the ground chewing on a thick wheat bread. Mom, a total wreck by now, was running all over the place with Milky in her lap. Once I gave her the message she sighed in relief and followed me to Jahir's house. At the sight of Rushi she couldn't stop the tears of joy that rolled down her cheek. Rushi however foolishly kept on smiling.

She suffered a stomach upset that very night. The flat bread that the locals made at home was delicious but I guess it was too much for the tender stomach of Rushi. She had to be on bed rest for the next couple of days. This incident did bring some good for mom. She met Fatima who with her friendly and cheerful manners quickly won over her. Soon she started to pick up sequence and bid works and knitting wools from Fatima. I found myself fascinated with knitting and helped mom during my leisurely moments, acquiring some expertise soon, especially knitting woollen strings. This was done using a wooden block with a hole in the middle and four nails placed apart in equal distance around the hole. The technique was to continue to wrap the wool around the nails at the top and have the string grow through the hole. Mom knitted a hat for Milky for the ensuing winter and I knitted the string for it.

In this far border land people were aware of the ongoing independence war of Bangladesh but they didn't have much reason to become too much concerned. Dad listened to B.B.C. and other media like that and tried to understand the current situation. Sometime he would get together with Uncles Altaf and Jafor and discussed quietly. From hearing pieces of talks what I understood was that the war was moving ahead in full force. The freedom fighters of Bangladesh were vehemently resisting the Pakistani army's aggression. They had better success near the Indian borders. India had strengthened its assistance toward Bangladesh. Pakistan had also increased its number of soldiers in the war zone. In various border areas they were exchanging shots with the Indian army. Nobody knew which way the war was going. I quietly prayed with all my heart so that nobody in Khulna and villages were hurt. Especially I worried about Rani apa. I wondered if worthless Bashir would try to harm her in any way.

Dad's winter military exercise started in September and continued until end of November. One morning he bid us byes and went along the border to another part of Baluchistan with his unit. Mom cried a lot. I was quite sad as well. Dad won't be coming back for a while. Before leaving he took me into his arms and said," Take care of your mom. She won't be able to handle both Rushi and Milky alone. You must give her a hand."

This new responsibility enhanced my sense of pride by manifold. I nodded seriously. Uncles Altaf and Jafor also went away for winter exercise. I won't lie, after that our life felt a lot free. Especially considering the fact that mom truly became so engaged managing both Rushi and Milky that she would barely have time or desire left to give me hard time. At every opportunity I grouped up with Bashar and Ratul and drifted into the surrounding areas. We would also party with Roushon bhai and Rushni apa. Roushon bhai taught us a few card games. We played them whenever we got together. I tried my best to keep it a secret from mom. Playing cards wasn't considered as an acceptable activity for kids and she might tell dad when he returned. I didn't want any unnecessary trouble.

In October we heard that the freedom fighters had increased their resistance by manifold. Pakistan also increased its military presence to 80 thousand. India hadn't joined the war directly but did everything to assist the freedom fighters who had their major camps in Tripura, Assam and West Bengal. Refugees from the war affected country continued to flood bordering India. Suddenly Pakistan army decided to send the Infantry battalion located in Chaman to Mirpur Khash, located in Sindh, near the border of Rajasthan, India. Dad was ordered to go with this battalion to cover medical needs. Before leaving for Mirpur Khash he came home for a short visit. Mom was devastated in the news and became sick. Dad had to put her on saline. Thankfully Aunts Nori and Asifa volunteered to take care of Milky and Rushi during this challenging time. Bed ridden and tearful mom repeatedly would ask, "Why are they sending you to war?"

"I am a doctor." Dad would explain patiently. "They are not sending me to war. I'll be going with the soldiers just to cover them medically. After we reach there, I'll come back. Why are you so worried?"

Mom didn't find much consolation. She continued to shed tears even after dad left. Rushi joined her sometime as usual. However, to everybody's surprise Milky remained in good spirit, smiling and giggling throughout the entire family crisis.

Dad's battalion moved ahead in a long caravan. It took them five – six days to reach Mirpur Khash. The trip went without any incidents. After reaching there, dad was asked to find his own unit. Dad was a member of 31st field ambulance. Fortunately his unit was nearby with another battalion. He joined them and stayed in Mirpur Khash until the next instruction came. In the mean time army decided to move all the families from Chaman to Quetta. Several of the families including us packed up and moved in army vehicles. We had no contact with dad in between. But we were told that all the officers who were away on duty will meet us in Quetta when they are released from their duties. Mom could barely wait. She stayed on the prayer mat most part of the day.

We were given housing inside Quetta cantonment – a specious house with two units. Roushon bhai and his family occupied the unit attached to ours. Ratul's family got a house far from us.

Chapter 13

I fell in love with the new house at the first sight. While the inside of the house was great – specious and everything, that wasn't the main reason of my excitement. It was the outside that I loved. The huge garden in front of the house consisted of several kind of fruit trees including apple, peach, apricot, grape and pears. There was also a rose garden in one side of the house. I was so excited that the only thing I left doing was performing a classical Indian dance. The apple trees were just flowering. I spent most of my time checking the trees, taking mental notes on their conditions, sizes etc. The apricot tree was quite large which I learned to scale. Rushni apa liked apricots. To ensure her continuous affection I filled up my pockets with apricots and delivered half of that to her. Apparently mom liked apricot too. But she was scared to let me climb the trees. However, after I showed her my newly earned skill she was pretty impressed.

There were two long grape vines that climbed onto our high boundary walls. Those were flowering as well. Rushi and I made time to examine them on regular basis. I never dreamt of getting such a wonderful garden almost like the one we had in the village in this exotic land. Very soon I forgot about losing Bashar and Ratul.

At the end of November dad had an opportunity to visit us in Quetta. He liked the house as well. Most of his life was spent in the villages. Greeneries moved him too. We had a large yard inside the boundary wall. During his short stay he prepared the soil and planted several pumpkin plants and sprinkled radish seeds. He heard from the locals that the earth here was good for pumpkins. It fell on my shoulder to water the plants and seeds and uproot the weeds. I loved gardening and spent large portion of my day either in the vegetable garden or in the fruit garden. Rushi would give me a hand sometimes too, depending on how she felt on a particular day. Milky had just turned five months. He kept all of us entertained with his baby talks. Lately he had been trying to crawl but no matter how much effort he put he wasn't going anywhere with his puffy body. He seemed to patronise me quite a bit, smiling whenever I came into his view. When the time came for dad to leave even he seemed a little sad. He held Milky a little longer than usual but didn't say anything. He left in an army vehicle. We walked behind the vehicle up to the main road. It was already getting a little cold. Seeing Milky shivering inside mom's lap we quickly returned home.

On December 3rd Pakistan abruptly attacked India by air on the ground that the later was providing unwanted assistance to East Pakistan. The very next day Indian government decided to send army to help East Pakistan. Until then prime minister of India Indira Gandhi had been hesitating to formally approve the war. This attack made her job simpler. The initial air attack that Pakistan conducted was unable to do much damage to India. Very soon they took control of the air. The army that India ended up sending to Bangladesh was consisted of nine infantry division with armour units and arms units. They divided into five branches and moved through Bangladesh very quickly. Their primary target was to reach Dhaka, the capital of then East Pakistan. On the way they avoided the small strongholds of the Pakistani armies.

In this journey their primary help came from the innumerable units of freedom fighters who engaged the Pakistani army units into small, consuming battles all over the country. Four of the army divisions belonging to Pakistan initially resisted the advance of Indian army strongly but eventually they started to break down. All the supply routes and escape routes chocked they had no other option but to surrender. On December 16th Dhaka fell. Commander of Pakistani army Lieutenant General A.A.K.Niaji surrendered to the Commander of the joined forces of Indian army and the freedom fighters of Bangladesh Lieutenant General J.S.Arora. On the west front the war that had initiated between India and Pakistan that didn't give any edge to Pakistan either.

In the news of independence the Bangladeshi community here became overwhelmed. Everybody was hoping to return home soon. Dad returned from the battle field almost immediately. There was no talk of getting us back to Bangladesh yet but having dad back made our lives pretty happy. Dad and I joined forces to clean our vegetable garden of weeds that grew abundant despite all my effort to stop their spread. The pumpkin plants had started to flower. The earth was clearly very fertile. In the apple garden the apple buds were turning into small apples. I made it my daily routine to walk around the garden and check on every tree. Rushi would accompany me most days. She had been showing unusual interest in nature since we moved in here.

Most of us hoped to return home without much delay. Such thoughts brought both happy and sad feelings to me. I was happy because it would allow me to see my relatives back home. The sadness came from the fact that I had already become so much attached to the gardens and the trees that I would miss them very much. If we had to leave too quickly we wouldn't be able to see neither the apples growing nor the pumpkins. Some people had already been questioning my mental stability noticing my devotion to those plants.

One day all soldiers and officers were called in a meeting in the Camp Coulee which was part of Quetta cantonment. Everybody was asked whether they desired to stay back in Pakistan or return to Bangladesh. A handful of men had married Pakistani women who opted to stay in Pakistan, the rest eagerly wanted to return. Pakistan government confirmed that everybody would return home though the schedule was not yet fixed. When Pakistan surrendered India took about 75000 soldiers as prisoners. Pakistan was trying to use the expatriate Bangladeshi soldiers and officers to bring back some of those prisoners. At this news mom again started to cry. Honestly, I was sort of happy. This would give me a few months. It was decided that everybody would continue to live in their current abode but the men would have to show up in an assembly once every day. The government didn't want anybody to escape.

December in Quetta was cold. Hail and snow both were possibilities. We started to feel the coolness to some extent. Every night three of us siblings took bathe in water that was warmed up using small dip in heaters. After bath mom would quickly wipe us dry, help us put on night dresses and sent us to the bed under the warm waiting blankets. Milky was about six months old and was a lot of fun. His excitement increased considerably at my sight, especially when I would open the front or back door and would allow him to crawl out in the yard. Sometimes I carefully picked him up in my lap and took him around the gardens. Mom didn't fill very comfortable about it fearing I might drop him. But Milky liked it so much that she was hesitant to stop me from doing it. Rushi often struggled to pick Milky up in her lap but she herself was so skinny that it was out of question. One time in her request I had put Milky on her lap. After just two shaky steps she fell on the ground with Milky rolling on her. Not sure where she was hurt but she did cry for a while. The good part was Milky had a blast in the process and giggled unstopped. Rushni apa and Roushan bhai both were big fans of Milky. Rushni apa took Milky with her in her frequent social trips into the neighbourhood. She met a few girls of her age in the area. Milky soon became very fond of her. We were really blessed having the two (Rushni apa and Roushan bhai) and really enjoyed all the affection and indulgence we received from them.

Amid all this one day I ended up doing something very undesirable. I had accompanied dad to the local store. It was night and the store did not have very bright lights. When dad was busy purchasing essentials I observed the glass cases where various sweets were neatly arranged for display on ceramic plates. They looked so tempting that at one opportunity I picked one up and put it in my mouth. However, soon I remembered dad had mentioned to me not to eat anything from a store without paying for it first. I was in trouble. I could neither chew it nor take it out, both of which were risky as either one of dad or the store owner might notice it. I placed the sweet in one corner of my mouth and stood innocently. I noticed the store owner smiling at me. I acted as if I had no clue. Anyway, dad eventually noticed the bulge in my mouth. "What is it in your mouth, Khoka?" He asked.

I kept quiet, naturally. The store owner laughed. "Don't worry about it. He is just a kid, got tempted."

Dad was mad. "If you wanted to eat it why didn't you ask me? Throw it out."

I threw it out. Dad bought some sweets to take back home with us. On our way back I looked down the entire path. Even I didn't know why I had done something so foolish. Dad remained grave serious. He was a man of principle and never took such lapses very well.

As we approached our house I muttered," I'll never do it again. They looked too good."

"That was stealing. Do not ever do it again. Are you going to remember that?"

I nodded. After reaching home I ate half of the sweets. "Why are you eating so many sweets?" Mom inquired. "You already have too many cavities."

I didn't respond to her. Luckily dad did not tell her about the incident in the store. It really saved me from a lot of agony. If she heard about it she would have made my life miserable for months bringing it up in every possible opportunity.

Almost before our eyes the pumpkins continued to grow larger and larger into sort of giants and the radishes became thicker and longer with the green leaves growing taller. This practically wiped out any doubt that we might have had about the fertility of the land here. The question now was what to do with all that harvest. We ate and distributed in the neighbourhood in plentiful but there was still much left.

The apples grew slowly but steadily. A few more days and they would ripe into delicious fruits. I tried out a few but they were still very green and tasted sour. The trees were mostly medium in size but they bore so many fruits that the branches leaned visibly toward the ground. I couldn't help but wonder what we would do with so many apples.

God must have taken my worries too seriously because a few days later suddenly one night there was a big hailstorm. I could barely sleep that night worrying about the apples. The hails would either detach the fruits or damage them. Next morning as soon as I woke up I ran to the apple garden along with my dad. We walked around to check on all the trees. The damage was far more than what I had anticipated. There was not a single apple that wasn't damaged. If we left them in the trees they would eventually rot. We decided to harvest all of them. Mom knew how to make good jelly.

For the rest of the day we filled out bushels with apples and carried them inside the house. The ones that we couldn't reach from the ground I quickly climbed up the trees and picked them up. Watching me running around busily Milky got really excited and tried to follow me into the garden on four. Mom picked him up ending his adventurous expedition. He screamed and cried in vein. Rushni Apa, Roushon bhai and their parents joined us in the garden as well. It turned out to be something like a festival. For the next few days mom cut the apples, separated the white flesh and boiled them in large pots. The whole place smelled strangely, not something very pleasant. Later she mixed up the broth with sugar and continued to heat it up until emitted the appetising smell of jelly. Later the jelly was poured into containers of all kind and shape. After distributing half of them what remained even that was enough for a year.

A new problem popped up in the beginning of January. A few Bangladeshi officers had escaped from another region. Pakistan government didn't like that. They took precaution to ensure that the folks who were staying in Quetta did not try anything foolish. Soon all the officers and their families were moved to hotel Jiltan located inside the cantonment which was used to host officers who came for training and the soldiers and their families were taken to Camp Coulie. Each of the officer's family was assigned a suite. Moving to a small hotel suite leaving behind such a beautiful house and garden made me very sad. The suite had two rooms with a small kitchen and a balcony. We were told that this arrangement was very temporary. Soon the government would move us all to another unspecified place. All together we were a few hundred families. The new place would have to be big enough to hold all of us.

Once the initial shock was over we kind of started to like it in the hotel, especially me, after realizing that this allowed me to get together with Bashar, Ratul and Moti again. We were also delighted to find out that there were at least six – seven other kids of our age in the camp. Our lives became exciting again. We packed up and played as long as we wanted. There was no schooling, little studies. Just play, play and play. The adults weren't having a bad time either, especially the dads. They still had to attend the daily roll call but after that they were free to do whatever they wanted. There was a field in front of the hotel with a volleyball ground at its center. Soon the men teamed up and started to play volleyball in the afternoons. The women gathered on the front balconies to either watch the men and kids play or just to chat with each others. There was definitely some advantage of living in such a close community.

Since coming to West Pakistan I didn't see such festive mode. We kids also copied the elders and tried to come up with our own sport experimenting with soccer, cricket, and hockey. Unfortunately there weren't enough space and none of the games stuck. Finally we got creative and collectively came up with the one deadly solution that everybody readily agreed to - the war games. We divided into two groups with Bashar, Ratul, Moti, Ranju, Ovi and I in one team and Tanna, Mishon, Mijan, Aman, Joti and Roni in the other. A few girls tried to join us but were not allowed. They tend to get tired quickly and were prone to start girlish conversations instead of battling it out. Nobody appreciated such childish behaviour in a serious matter like a war. Our rifles were branches, rocks grenades, a light post in front of the hotel became the war bell. The game started with several bangs on the light post – dong, dong, dong...and continued until one of the teams got tired or surrendered.

Every afternoon when men went to play volleyball, we got busy fighting mock battles. Often hours would pass and none of the teams would give up. We rattled rat-a-tat-tat...dashed for shelter...hid behind the trees...dived inside holes on the ground...more rat-a-tat-tat...threw grenades...kaboom! Almost every day we had to be yelled at and forced into our homes, often by the ears. Soon we became skilled soldiers and knew all the hiding places in the hotel premise like the back of our hands. We also introduced battle plans and spent hours plotting strategy to beat our opponent. I was the self proclaimed commander-in-chief in my team while Aman with his heavy set body easily became the chief of the other team. He was the only son of Uncle Syed and Aunt Misha and was slightly older than us. He was quieter and a little weird. Everybody avoided unnecessary encounters with him, fearing that getting into trouble with him couldn't be anything pleasant.

Mothers soon reigned in our freedom and drastically increased our study times. We were no more allowed to go out in the mornings. As a result we eagerly waited for the afternoons. Once the sun leaned toward the west and the day started to cool off slowly the men made their way out to the field in small groups, opening the door for us to go out. We bolted out at the first opportunity, competed among us to bang the war bell ...dong...dong... dong... and got engaged into fierce battles ...screaming and rat-tling...running around like loose cannons.

I met Aman after moving in Hotel Jiltan. For reasons unclear to me we didn't hit the right notes. We settled as rivals instead. When we came face to face we glared at each other and barely spoke. Since we started to play war games our relationship had deteriorated even further. Now when we saw each other we actually frowned. The conversations went something like this:

"Yesterday we won." Aman would gravely de-clare.

"Don't be silly. I killed all of you with my ma-chinegun." I would disregard his claim with disgust.

"No way! I blew all of you with my bombs." He would insist, aggressively.

After such exchanges naturally the excite-ment ran high in the battle field. None of us wanted to leave any doubt about the outcome. During the battles I led my team through the battle field attack-ing the enemy with spraying bullets rat-a-tat-tat....Aman's primary strategy was to hide behind the trees and throw bombs constantly. Initially he threw mock bombs which quickly became small rocks. As the rivalry increased between us the size of the rocks grew bigger as well. It did not worry any of us. The dangerous the enemy the more was the fun. We dashed from shelter to shelter avoiding the bombarding rocks that Aman and his team kept on showering at us. When somehow we made it behind them without being detected a sudden 'Hands Up!' cleanly made us the winner.

After losing out a few consecutive times Aman must have felt very embarrassed because he resorted to extreme measures. Nobody had any idea what mischievous plan he was plotting. One day as we played out our regular battles I followed my usual strategy and hid into my favourite ditch shooting relentlessly rat-a-tat-tat....The bullets were sprayed at such a rate that there was no question of any enemy soldiers approaching me, as they would definitely get shot. However, today Aman broke the rule. He ignored all the shootings and bombings directed at him and walked straight to me with his assortments of rocks acting as grenades.

"Aman you are dead." I screamed after spraying him with another round of deadly bullets. "Drop down."

"No, I am not dead." Aman shouted back stubbornly. "I am wearing a bullet proof vest."

Before I had an opportunity to object he started pelting rocks at me. I successfully avoided some by diving low but wasn't fast enough to move out of the way of a large rock that got me right on the middle of the forehead. It didn't hurt much but I saw blood gushing out in a stream. I knew I was wounded. Dad was in the field playing volleyball. I climbed out of the ditch and darted toward him leaving behind a streak of blood. Aman had already disappeared. Rest of the boys followed me to the ground. Dad came rushing at me, picked me up in his lap and ran toward the hotel. The boys and some of the men followed us to the suite. Dad laid me down on a bed and stitched my wound. The cut was relatively big and required six stitches. After losing considerable amount of blood I felt really weak and drowsy. However that didn't stop mom from berating me. "How many times did I tell you not to play that game? How about now? If I see you playing again I am going to break your head myself."

My friends quickly disappeared. Dad didn't return to play. He sat by me and took my temperature in regular interval. Rushi parked herself at a safe distance and watched me cautiously. She had no stomach for blood. I called her several times but she made no attempt to move closer. Milky was the happiest. When I went out to play with my friends he stayed back with mom, not something he appreciated. Now that I was stuck inside the home he spent most of his time crawling and drooling over me. His joy had lessened some of my pain.

Next few days I had to stay inside the house. Any attempt to step out met severe warnings and screaming from mom. Bashar and Ratul had come to see me but terrified of mom they didn't dare to knock on the door and left after waiting sometime in the corridor. I could hear them whispering. Our war games had stopped. Everybody heard about the misdeed of Aman. His parents had put him under house arrest as well.

"He should face court martial." I demanded to dad.

Dad smiled. "Both of you should face court martial. There are so many sports and you guys have to play war games?"

I couldn't answer him. How could I possibly explain to him how thrilling and exciting it was.

A few days later, Aman and his parents visited us one evening. Uncle Syed and Aunt Misha were kind and affectionate people. Aunt Misha brought me some sweets that she made herself. I devoured them. The best part came when both of them demanded that Aman formally apologized to me. Aman put on a nasty frown on his face, stubbornly looked down on the ground and robotically recited, "Sorry. It was a mistake. I'll never do it again."

His mom prompted him to say some additional stuff which he didn't even attempt to. No amount of scolding or pleading made Aman open his mouth again. Frustrated his parents said many kind things and promised to come see me again before pulling Aman away.

My parents ruled that until my stitches completely healed I wouldn't be allowed to go out. As a result I had to spend my afternoons in the balcony. Bashar, Ratul, Joti, Roni and others played hide and seek. They didn't let Aman play with them for several days. Aman used to stand all by himself. After I urged Ratul he was allowed in. I thought after that we would become friends but in reality he continued to hold grudge against me.

In the mean time something much serious happened. A few days later one afternoon mom went to visit the neighbouring suite taking Milky along with her. I was sitting in the balcony watching the regular activities on the ground. Kids were running around as usual. Men grouped up and just started playing volleyball. Dad went to play after missing a few days. I noticed that the men had two teams with fixed members who faced each other every day. In one team belonged dad along with Uncles Syed, Bajlur, Jafor and Joti's dad, Roni's dad and two other officers. The other team was consisted of Uncle Altaf, Captain Sujon, Major Nayeem, Shirin's dad, Ovi's dad, Ranju's dad and other two officers. In total eight players in each team. Someday additional players came in who were randomly distributed between the two teams. Most of the officers were captains and majors but there were a few colonels as well. In dad's team only Uncle Jafor was a major, rest of them captains. In Uncle Altaf's team he and Uncle Nayeem were majors and the rest captains. Captain Sujon who played in his team was very noisy and temperamental. Most had already seen him losing his cool a few times. However, things had never gone too far primarily because nobody wanted unnecessary trouble.

Today I noticed Captain Sujon was pointing a finger at dad and was speaking aggressively. Dad was generally very calm person but when mad he could get out of control. Soon I realized he was engaged in an argument with Captain Sujon. Most probably it was about scoring a point. Dad had carefully left alone a service ball served by Captain Sujon which bounced outside of the playing area. However Captain Sujon would not accept that and insisted that the ball actually bounced inside the court. Members of both teams sincerely tried to resolve the issue but for whatever reason things went out of hand. Eventually the argument spread out among others and soon two teams engaged into a shouting match. The sudden turn of events took everybody in such shock that the children stopped playing and the women hurried out. The argument turned uglier and a skirmish broke down. Major Jafor and Captain Sujon got into a fist fight. At one point Captain Sujon pulled a knife out of his pocket and attacked Major Jafor with it. Uncle Altaf reached out and held him tightly in a lock immobilizing him.

"I'll arrange for your court martial." Uncle Jafor shouted. "You'll be returning to Bangladesh, won't you?"

Several women had run to the ground. They tried to pull away their husbands from the field. I saw mom bolting toward dad with Milky still in her lap. Uncles Bajlur and Syed had already pushed dad out of the field. Mom held his hand and stubbornly pulled him in the suite. Still too agitated dad stepped out in the balcony and continued to yell at his opponents.

The situation in the ground had improved considerably by now. A few men held back Captain Sujon while many others had already returned to their homes. It took another few hours before peace returned. But the impact of this event continued for several days. The trouble in the volleyball ground touched our social lives as well. Uncle Altaf and dad were very good friends but after that incident their relationship turned cold. They only exchanged stiff pleasantries when faced each other. The volleyball game had also stopped for a little while.

In the mean time, my stitches were opened. There was a clearly visible scar on the forehead, which I thought gave me something to be proud of. After all it was received during a battle, mock or not. That afternoon stepping out after weeks I banged on the light post with a fist sized rock dong...dong...dong...At first a few of the boys came out curiously. Soon we called out the rest, even Aman, collectively agreed not to use any rocks and started the battle in full force. A few days later the men were back in the volleyball ground however captain Sujon was nowhere to be seen.

At the end of January a decision was taken to send us all to fort Sandaman.

Chapter 14

The small town called Fort Sandaman was located in the valley of Jobe. The word Jobe meant stream of water. The name reflected the fact that it was the source of the river Jobe. A part of Baluchistan this region was on the north-east border of Pakistan and Afghanistan. This valley was famous for its mountainous geography and historical value in whole of Pakistan. This valley begun from Muslimbag, a place 7500 feet above the sea level and ended in Fort Sandaman, 10000 feet above sea level. The town was named after Sir Robert Sandaman who established the rule of British Empire in this region. He was the political agent of the Governor General of Baluchistan in 1890. This town was located about three hundred kilometres away from Quetta. (* Today it is called Jobe. In 1976 July 30th Zulfikar Ali Bhutto changed the name of Fort Sandaman to Jobe.)

We rode the train once again. Another memorable trip! We passed through mountains after mountains and tunnels after tunnels on our way to Fort Sandaman. It was a small town surrounded by pine forests. We were placed inside the cantonment. There were inadequate officers housing hence two families had to share the same house. Major Yunus's family and our family shared a two bedroom house. Uncle Yunus had two sons – Tanna and Mijan. We were three siblings. It was very difficult for one family to live in just one room. Dad applied for new housing. He was informed that in the officer's housing there was no other vacancy however in the GCO housing there were. Dad readily accepted it. We packed up again, bid farewell to Tanna and Mijan and moved to the GCO quarter nearby. This house was also a two bedroom unit but we had it all by ourselves. Dad and mom sighed in relief. They occupied one room with Milky sleeping with them, Rushi and I took the other. We got our own beds. Rushi was a bad sleeper and continued to fall from his bed almost every night. Sometimes she managed to get back on the bed, some other mornings we found her curled up on the floor. This soon became a cherished joke among us. Milky had started to crawl. He looked very happy in the new house.

The houses here were built in rows with tilted roofs. A road ran across just ahead. Tall light posts flanked it on both sides. Officer's quarter was only a few minutes' walk. I used to walk down there very often to play with Bashar and Ratul. Roushon bhai and Rushni apa's family got a specious house. I visited them whenever an opportunity came. Dad and Uncle Altaf still hadn't completely warmed up. However, their coldness did not have any impact on the kid's. Very often Roushon bhai and Rushni apa walked us home.

One day with pure shock I discovered that Aman's family occupied a house very close to ours.

Since he injured me our relationship had remained cold. We played together but barely spoke. Being forced to come to our house and apologize to me must have been very embarrassing to him because every time he saw me his face turned dark.

Since we moved to Fort Sandaman our war games were on hold primarily because it was winter here. This region could get pretty cold and heavy snowfall was a usual thing. We were from tropical region, not accustomed to severe cold. Many of us suffered from cold and cough on regular basis. Nevertheless we bolted out at every opportunity we got. The temptation to play outdoors with friends was too strong to be held back by petty weather. On my regular visits to Officer's housing I started to meet Aman quite frequently. It didn't take me too long to figure out that Aman planned it that way. Against all odds we soon became good friends though I had to initiate the process. One day as he silently walked with me to the officer's quarters I stopped. "Let's be friends." I proposed.

Aman twisted his lips and observed me thoughtfully. Finally he nodded approvingly. We curved our pointers and held them briefly together like hooks. We now became committed to a lifelong friendship.

"My forehead is fine now." I said casually.

Aman smiled quietly. He wasn't very good with words but his smiles were meaningful. It clearly told me that he was very happy.

Next afternoon it snowed a little. The rolling hills, tilted roofs, asphalt roads everything became covered in white snow. Mom had cautioned me earlier not to go out in that weather. I had nothing much to do and was quite bored at home. I wondered what Aman was doing. Mom was keeping a close eye fearing I might ignore her warning and slipped out of the house. Suddenly I heard a loud bang ...dong...dong...dong...somebody was using a rock to bang on the light post – the war bell! Mom heard that as well. "Step outside and I'll break your legs." She issued a stern warning.

Helpless and unhappy I stomped inside the house restlessly. Dad chuckled. "Let him go for a little bit. Don't go too far."

"You indulge him too much." Mom shot back. "He slips out as he wishes. Doesn't listen to anything I say."

I bolted out of the door before dad changed his mind. Stepping out I got a pleasant surprise. All the boys from officer's housing including Bashar and Ratul had come and Aman was diligently banging the war bell. We didn't waste any time. Two teams were formed quickly and the game started - once again. The only difference this time was that Aman and I belonged to the same team. Pretty soon with all our shouting and screaming we shook up the neighbourhood.

We didn't play every day. Sometimes Aman and I walked aimlessly in the surrounding areas. It became one of our favourite activities. Often we met the locals. They waived affectionately, sometimes made small conversations. Every time we went in new direction. Occasionally even Rushi joined us with her favourite doll in her lap. Many of the soldiers knew us. "Boys, don't go too far." They gravely warned. "Go back home before its dark." We adhered to those rules anyway. First of all, getting back late would mean relentless scolding from mom; secondly, both of us were more or less scared of darkness.

There was no school here. We were all being home schooled. Dad and mom suddenly started to push both Rushi and me harder into studies. They feared that once we returned home we would be behind considerably than other kids of our age. At this point our lives became quite difficult. I heard that everybody was pondering to start a temporary school inside the confinement for the expatriate Bangladeshis. To find proper books and eligible teachers for the older kids could be difficult but getting something going for the younger kids like us was relatively easy. However, owing to various issues the school didn't materialize during the winter months. We were very excited about the school. Under normal conditions getting out of the house before afternoon was hard for all of us. With the school open we could spend a major portion of the day away from the hawk eyes of our parents. We weren't too crazy about studying but we were ready to take it for some freedom.

In the mean time dad found a hafiz (a religious scholar) among the soldiers. He was about
24/25 and grew up in Khulna. He had memorized the
Qur'an to its entirety. A cheerful person in nature he
taught kids how to read Arabic and eventually the
Qur'an. I liked him for his carefree nature. His name
was Mohammed Meher, we called him Meher bhai.
He called mom aunt and quickly became an integral
part of our family. He taught Rushi and me how to
read Arabic. Rushi got stuck on the alphabets while I
quickly passed through the intermediate stages and
started to read Qur'an. Though I didn't understand
the meaning of the words but I learned to read it
very well. Meher bhai tried to teach me how to recite Qur'an but I had no interest in that. All I wanted
was to finish reading the Qur'an at least once and
stunt my friends many of who were struggling to finish Ampara, the intermediary step.

Meher bhai used to teach Bashar and Ratul
Arabic as well and both were stuck in Ampara. He felt
they were not paying much attention. I on the other
hand continued to surprise him, according to him,
with my hard work as I read through half of a chapter
in one sitting, not a simple task for a novice reader by
any means. What he didn't know was a little secret
that worked like steroid for me. My parents had
promised me to arrange for a milad muhfil (a religious gathering) to celebrate my completion of
Qur'an where all my friends along with their families
would be invited. Just the thought of everybody com-

ing under the same roof to acknowledge one of my great accomplishments gave me goose bumps.

Few days later we received a letter from Dadu. This was the first letter since independence. Dadu wrote that they were safe and sound in the village. After the robbery attempt things had been pretty quiet. The dacoits were never caught. Everybody was fine in nana's house as well. Knowing my especial concern he specifically mentioned about Rani apa. She could not go to Khulna and stayed back in the village during the war. The worthless Bashir apparently joined a unit of freedom fighters and was killed in an operation. His death was sort of suspicious as nobody saw the dead body. Dadu cast his doubt about him really joining the war. Chachu and his family were okay in Satkhira. They had suffered no damages. To his best knowledge khala and khalu were doing just fine in Khulna.

We were all very much relieved, especially me. The news of Bashir dying came as a pleasant surprise. I had no doubt Allah was beating the hell out of him. That's what you get for eve teasing. Dad and mom arranged for a religious gathering where one or several persons would recite the Quran from start to end. Meher bhai decided to recite it all alone throughout the day. As a Hafez he had the Quran memorized. The event created big commotion in the kid's circle. How could anybody memorize such a large book when we had tough time remembering tiny verses! Everybody came to see him reciting from memory. In the evening when the recitation finally completed mom offered everybody her homemade sweet balls and galebi. Her galebi turned out reasonably good but the sweet balls often came out kind of hard. Today was no exception. However, everybody gorged on them anyway.

The winter passed by eventually. Here the summer was hot but not as humid which made it kind of bearable. After a lot of trouble finally a school was established for the kids. There was a single storied building near the officer's housing which was converted into the school. Initially it started with only three grades – two, three and four. Even though I had completed all the grade two books at home I had to be admitted in grade two because of my age. The only other student in my class was Ratul. Rest of the boys who came to attend the school were slightly older than two of us. Most of them were put in grade three with a handful in grade four. This was the first time ever for me and Ratul in a school. We both loved it especially the short recesses after every lesson. We all poured out in the field and kicked around a soccer ball until call for the next lesson came.

In grade two our teacher was a young woman named Nabiha Khan. She was very pretty and kept herself well. She spoke softly and smiled frequently. When she spoke both Ratul and I listened eagerly. We competed against each other to become her object of affection. We raced to finish our class works ahead of the other. Fortunately I beat Ratul most of the time. When she smiled beautifully at me and said in her pleasant voice," Good work Khoka!" my world became so much better. Sometimes if Ratul was sick I was sent to grade three. I hated those days. I wanted to be in Miss Nabiha's class. Eventually Ratul and I learned to share this wonderful gift between us. Miss Nabiha must have guessed something fishy was going on noticing our constant nudges and whisperings because I found her chuckling every now and then. Talk about embarrassment!

Time passed by in Fort Sandaman. While the kids had considerably good time with school and sports the adults were more or less bored. My parents were anxious to go back home. How long could one remain stuck in a foreign land? I noticed dad looked worried sometimes. The new prime minister of Bangladesh was naturally Sheikh Mujibur Rahman. He returned to Bangladesh on 19th January 1972 after being released from the Pakistani prison. At first he occupied the position of the president but later resigned and accepted the position of the prime minister. On 4th November same year Bangladesh created its first constitution in the same form of British styled Indian constitution. All the news that we received gave us an impression that the situation in Bangladesh could take a while to settle down. Many freedom fighters did not give up their weapons after the independence. Many joined the Bangladesh army and occupied higher ranks too quickly. Dad and other officers who were stuck in Pakistan feared that when they returned home they won't get their fitting ranks. It was their misfortune that they became stuck in West Pakistan and did not have the opportunity to participate in the war for Bangladesh. They believed officers who were juniors to them would grab this opportunity to embarrass them. I could make out from his expressions that he was seriously pondering of quitting army once he returned home. However returning to Bangladesh seemed a distant option. Pakistan was using us to have India release the large number of soldiers and officers it took as prisoners. Exchanging prisoners wasn't an easy thing especially when this was done with a third country. There were also many Biharis stranded in Bangladesh who wanted to return to Pakistan. Overall quite a complex situation. Things seemed to move very slowly in the political arena. We knew unless things started to go much faster our chances of going back home too soon were an unrealistic one.

Mom planted some vegetable in the small patch of land attached to the house. I lend her a hand whenever possible. Milky had turned a year old. He was power crawling and had started to stand up on his own. He was already trying to follow me everywhere. If I went outside he would scream to go with me. If I went to the garden he would also crawl to the garden. Helpless I had to pick him up in my lap or he would plough through the plants. Aman became very fond of him. He had no siblings. He must have felt very lonely at home because he frequently visited our house. Mom liked him for his quiet and calm nature. Later he even joined us in Arabic class. However Meher bhai was not impressed with his progress and often teased him. "Aman, are you reading Bengali or Arabic?"

Aman was determined not to get discouraged. Meher bhai was a patient man. He tried hard to help him pick it up. My progress, on the other hand, started to make both my parents and Meher bhai suspicious. They did not appreciate my fast pace. Could it be that I wasn't reading properly? May be I was making a lot of mistakes. They hinted at many things. I remained motivated ignoring all criticisms.

The short summer raced by as the winter was approaching fast. I still had several chapters to read and was starting to have serious doubts about meeting my goal. The final test in school was also coming up. We learned that the first boy or girl in every grade would get a reward. Beating Ratul didn't seem like a problem at all. I was already speculating about the nature and size of the reward that I was going to receive.

In this mountainous region winter came abruptly. Before we knew the summer was gone. The feeling of coolness felt sort of good in the beginning of winter but later things became shivering cold. Every morning Aman and I walked to the school all wrapped up in warm cloths. I was in grade two, Aman grade three.

Miss Nabiha prepared the question papers for the final exam. She explained repeatedly the full syllabus of our ensuing tests. There will be two tests – English and Maths. Her question papers were usually easy. The thought of receiving the prize from her hand sounded so luring that I studied very well. Ratul and I sat side by side on the same bench and wrote the tests. Miss Nabiha sometime sat in front of us, sometime stepped out to get fresh air.

The English test went very well for both of us. We answered all the questions correctly. Ratul was good in English. His problem was maths. I had strong belief that in maths I would have no problem beating him. Once I looked at the question paper I could not stop smiling. It was so easy! Even Ratul looked very relaxed. However, around the end he faced some difficulties. When Miss Nabiha stepped out he asked for my help. The thought of not helping a friend never occurred in my mind. I, rather foolishly, showed him everything he needed. What a catastrophe! When the results came out I found out that I scored 1 point less in English than Ratul. We both scored same points in Maths. Ratul was first, me second.

On the day when Miss Nabiha brought the huge wrapped up gift to Ratul's house I was playing in the vicinity. She waved at me. I waved back dryly. Finally it was Ratul who won. I didn't have to help him with maths. I shook the thought out of my mind quickly. He was my friend and helping him was the right thing to do. Who cared about a stinky award? Aman read my mind. He approved, in his own way. "This is a worthless prize. Let's go for a walk." I quietly followed him.

My parents had much more difficulty in accepting it. None of them had any doubt that I secured the first position. Recently news were being leaked that the kids whose parents were in the governing body of the school were receiving undue favours, especially from the teachers. I found it difficult to believe that Miss Nabiha would intentionally give me low score. In English I was generally better than Ratul but perhaps I didn't do as well in this particular test. May be I did a few silly mistakes. My being second had nothing to do with Ratul's dad being a member of the governing body. But it was difficult to explain that to my parents especially mom. The suspicion became so strong that next year I wasn't sent to school any more. I was being home schooled. I had no desire to leave the joyous environment of the school and stay home but there wasn't much I could do. I saw my friends in the afternoon. Recently we stopped playing war games and started to play soccer. Who knew there was so much pleasure in chasing a ball around! My skill grew fast. Soon I became a key player in the group.

One night in the wee hours a sudden loud noise woke me up. Dad and mom woke up too. Dad looked outside through the windows to figure out what might have happened. That didn't help much as none of the windows in our house had a clear view of the road. But we agreed that it sounded like a car skidding and hitting something. "Could be an accident." Dad said. "You guys go to bed. I'll go check."

I wanted to go with him but mom stopped me. Disheartened I went back to bed. I thought of staying awake until dad returned but I was tired and soon went back to sleep. In the morning after waking up I slipped out of the house. Aman was coming this way. I learned from him that the commander himself had a car accident the night before. We ran toward the street. After looking around for a little bit we found the spot. The wreckage of the car had already been moved but the sign of the accident was very prominent on the lamp post where it happened.

That night I had a bloody nightmare. Screaming at the top of my voice I woke everybody up in the household. Mom was merciless. "Did you go to check out the accident site? Did you?" She screamed. "No wonder you are having nightmares. Didn't I ask you not to? One more screams and I'll slap the crap out of you."

I dipped inside the blanket and tried to sleep. I used to see a lot of dreams but not scary ones. This really freaked me out.

Finally at the end of March 1973 I completed reading Qur'an for the first time. Still suspicious about the quality my parents arranged for the celebration anyway. Mom prepared her famous galebi and hard sweet balls. Dad bought some stuff from the market as well. Meher bhai lead the milad muhfil with every bit of his heart. All the boys had come though not all of their parents did. I was noticing as the days passed by the kids were gradually learning to stop quibbling and to be friends while the grown-ups were getting more divided. It was becoming difficult for us to keep track of the bickering parents who weren't in talking terms.

Roushon bhai and Rushni apa came in the milad but Uncle Altaf and Aunt Nuri didn't. After that fight in the volleyball ground the relationship between the adults never really went back to the way it was before. Since Ratul secured first position the interaction between my parents and Uncle Bajlur and Aunt Saleha turned cold too. But I wasn't to be bothered with those tiny details. I was happy to see all my friends in the milad. We screamed at the top of our voice 'Yea nobi salam alaika' (salute to you dear prophet) with Meher bhai. I felt quite proud knowing that my friends were looking at me little differently at my achievement. Meher bhai was so happy that he bought a hat for me.

However, there was a by-product of this that made my life little painful. My parents started to push me to pray. Dad sometimes insisted me to join him in a group prayer. I obliged. However, after each prayer I raised my hands to Allah and prayed for toys and picture books. And surprisingly Allah listened to me and left small toys and occasionally story books under my pillow. That was probably the beginning of my reading habit. The few books that I received were written in easy English. I read them many times. Soon I noticed that Allah wasn't paying heed to my prayers any more. As a result my interest in prayer diminished too.

Chapter 15

Finally in August 1973 India and Pakistan signed a formal prisoner exchange agreement. India would release the 'Prisoner of wars' in exchange of all the stranded Bangladeshi army personnel and civilians. Worried and uncertain about the situation back home dad and mom still were overjoyed with the prospect of going back home. I on the other hand became truly sad in the thought of losing all my friends. Aman wasn't too happy either. One day we walked quietly along the street for a while.

"Where are you going to live once back home?" On our way back Aman asked.

I heard my parents discussing it. Dad would have to join Dhaka cantonment upon his return. If the working condition was not good then he planned to retire and start his own private practice in Dhaka. I explained it to Aman. Apparently his father was thinking in the same line. Still both of us knew once in Dhaka we weren't going to be able to see each other the way we did here. We probably would be living far away and if lucky may meet once in a blue moon. Dhaka was a big city, a crowded city.

Around the end of November we packed up our stuff and joined several others in boarding a train. We would go to Karachi first, from there fly to Dhaka. Ratul and his family were going in the same train with us. Aman would go a few days later. He came to the train station with his dad to say good bye. Right before the train started, he shyly murmured," I am sorry I hurt you."

I embraced him dearly and gave a broad smile. "Dad said the scar on my forehead won't go away too soon. That means I won't forget you that quickly."

Aman rarely smiled but on this moment his face lit up with an innocent smile. I waved at him and jumped back into the train. Soon the train moved forward. After two years we left our temporary homes, memories and a thousand small things behind us as the train headed toward Quetta. From Quetta to Karachi, then Dhaka. Who knew how life will be in Dhaka? I understood the anxiety of my parents. My concern was something else. I lost so many good friends in one shot, will I make any more? Who knew where we'll end up living? Would there be other boys? The joyous and carefree life that I was leaving behind, would I ever get it back? Milky was two years old. He ran around and spoke many words. He fondly called out for me 'Bhaiya! Bhaiya!" (bhaiya is a term for older brother) and flanked with me all the time. I liked it very much. I truly enjoyed the feelings of having a little brother.

Our train ran past beautiful mountainous region ... march on... march on... march on... march...march...march...I heard the melody of a famous song by Nazrul. I had already memorized a few of his melodious songs and poems. I sang out loudly as the rhythmic sound of the moving train became my music

March on, march!

The drum resounds in the sky above,

The earth below is all agog,

You the corps of youth of the scarlet dawn

March on, march on!

Milky would join me too enjoying every bit of it so much that he couldn't wipe off the babyish smile from his cute face. Rushi sat in mom's lap hanging dearly to her doll through this musical extravaganza. She had become very close to Milky as well. She even let him play with her favourite dolls. If anybody else had done so all hell would break loose.

Chuga... chuga... chuga... chuga... choo... choo...we advanced through the series of ridges and valleys, rolling hills, dark caves, dry lands, green fields...all of it seemed like the words of a lullaby... so melodious that it reverberated into the ears. Our parents were getting a little bit impatient in the long trip. On our way to Quetta from Karachi we were given first class accommodation. This time we were travelling on regular compartments, the comfort wasn't there. Mom had brought food for the way which was all we were eating. Dad had very little money left with him. We would need that once in

Dhaka. He didn't want to spend even a penny unless absolutely necessary.

Once we went past Quetta the hills started to disappear. The natural plain land of the province Sindh unfolded a different view in front of our eyes. The greeneries constantly fell behind us as we zoomed through green fields and occasional dwellings. Milky and I joined forces to run inside the compartment. Mom reprimanded but we continued. There was a sense of liberation in the air, as if this magical chariot of ours were carrying us away from the worldly limitations and bindings to a new world.

During long stoppages we hopped out to the station platform. Mom had also packed some rice and lintel like many others. She along with several other women lighted up small kerosene stoves and quickly cooked something up. It felt like a picnic. We were a happy bunch. Even Rushi was so excited that she went on to ask mom," Are we having a picnic, mom?"

Mom snapped at her. "Yes, picnic my foot!"

None of us could figure out why she was in such a bad mode. Dad tried to lighten the situation up by playing with us. Bashar and Ratul were travelling in a compartment at the other end of the train. We bunched up on the station. However dad and Uncle Jafor did not speak to each other. Many other kids joined us on the platform as well. We played 'tag' noisily. Even Milky joined us in the game though he kept on falling down on his butt. I was amazed to see him running around. He was just a tiny baby on our way to Quetta! Everybody in Bangladesh would be so surprised to see him.

The train started its journey again. We ate hot Khicuri made with rice and lintel. Mom seemed to get touched with our enthusiasm. She lightened up with a smile. "You kids are acting like this is some kind of festival."

We laughed cheerfully. How would mom know the pleasure in riding a train into the un-knowns? Could it be that the aging process took away the sense of magical feelings from mom? Slowly the sun disappeared in the horizon and came down the dusk like a mysterious sheet and the dark sky opened up the magical door to the moon and the stars. Soon, full and tired, we fell asleep. The train kept on going like a dark horse constantly humming in our ears ...sleep on...sleep on...I dreamt about my beloved ones...jhima, dadu, dadi, khala, khalu, cha-chi, chachu, Rani Apa, Minu Apa...so many oth-ers...even in the dreams I felt the eagerness to see them once again. I sent waves and waves of thoughts in the air ...we are coming Rani apa. Just a little longer.

Chapter 16

After we reached Karachi we stayed overnight in the Cantonment of Mali. We could not stay with Ayesha Apa and Jaman dulabhai this time. They were preparing to leave too. Their flight date was to be set later as they were civilians. Dad took permission to leave the cantonment to see them. Our flight was scheduled next day. This time we were allowed to fly over India cutting short the total travel time by quite a bit. Last time when we flew Milky was only a baby and had screamed our heads off, however this time around things were just opposite. He must have had mistaken the plane as a playground. It became really difficult to keep him constrained in his seat. He climbed down and ran up and down the aisle causing considerable amount of annoyance among some passengers. Rushi threw up twice. Dad was ready for something like this and no accidents happened. What I was surprised to notice that I had grown some sort of fear of height. This wasn't something that I was aware of before. Not sure how I got it but I couldn't even look out the window for most part of the flight.

I was about to doze off when the plane landed in Dhaka International airport. As I opened my eyes a glimpse of series of brick buildings and matured trees greeted me. It all felt so beautiful and personal. Even though I had never lived in Dhaka but still I had these amazing feeling of belonging to this city, this land. Mom was tearful. Not sure why. Dad smiled and said," Finally back to home."

In Dhaka we didn't have any close relatives. Doctor Asfak of Khulna had several brothers living in Dhaka. One of them was Uncle Mustak, who was a reputed engineer. He and his family came to receive us at the airport. We were very eager to go to Khulna and see our relatives but dad had to join in his job first. Once things settled down for him at work he could take a few days off and we would be able to make the trip to Khulna. I was eagerly counting days.

We stayed with Uncle Mustak's family for a few days in their house in Bhuter Goli. They had three children. Inti apa, Akash bhai and Shokash. Inti apa was a few years older than me and very affectionate. We liked her very much. Six kids in the same house – our days just flew by.

Dad applied for vacation almost immediately after joining in his job. His application was accepted and he was given a month off. We packed up our stuff again and got into a bus to Khulna the next day. Our plan was to stay in Khulna briefly and then go to Satkhira. After staying there one or two days we would go to the village.

It took us more than twelve hours to reach Khulna. The familiar view of the beautiful town dotted with coconut trees came as a big relief. Spending days in a train never felt boring or painful but sitting

in the crammed space of a bus for so long was un-
bearable. Especially the smell of Rushi's vomit was
sickening. Considering our long travel plan I sort of
felt pity for her. Throwing up wasn't a pleasant thing
to do. The only person who showed no sign of tired-
ness or annoyance was Milky. Every few seconds he
came up with all these absurd questions and mercilessly bombarded us with them. We took two rick-
shaws from the Khulna bus stand. The pullers knew
where khalu lived. In a town of this size reputed doctors, lawyers and politicians were known by almost
everybody.

Our arrival in khala's house stirred things up
quite a bit. They already knew we were coming.
When we reached we found half the neighbourhood
had gathered there. Mom hugged khala and broke
into tears. Rushi, scared of the crowd, grabbed
mom's saree and started crying as well. I only saw
Milky for a moment since we climbed down the rick-
shaws before the waiting crowd snatched him away.
He was born in this house so naturally everybody had
a special soft corner for him.

The house hadn't changed much in the last
few years. Though khalu hadn't been a supporter of
independence he didn't fully object to it either. Instead by chairing the local peace committee he had
saved the life of many people. Possibly that's why he
had no trouble after the war. In addition when Roni
bhai returned in one piece after the war ended the
honour of this family went sky high. However, I

learned from khala that like many other freedom fighters Roni bhai was unable to receive any reward or privilege from the government after the war.

Roni bhai didn't look much different. The card games went on as usual in the roof top den. Moni bhai looked his normal self. He cracked jokes every now and then and everybody burst into laughter. Parvoti's mom didn't like the extra effort that she had to put to make and carry tea and snacks for the gang. She was complaining all the time. I got confirmed news that Yunus did join the war. Roni bhai saw him in one of the training centers. However, he did not come back after the war ended. Khalu checked with his parents in the village. He did not go back there either. Nobody knew if he was killed in the war.

We stayed only one day in Khulna. My parents were anxious to see their folks. They were very eager to go to the village as soon as possible. Even I felt a strange pull for the meandering dirt roads, the huts with thatched roofs and the tree lined shadowy ponds – I missed all of them. Never before had I felt such strong feelings for the village. The urge that I felt to get together with my grandparents, jhima and Rani apa was something that cannot be expressed in words. I could still hear the melodious tune that Alek played in his bamboo pipe. How was he? When he see me would he come running as always and hug me and say,"How are you Khoka? Why so late?"

The distance between Khulna and Satkhira wasn't too much but it took six hours due to the local nature of the service. We were annoyed to the core but totally helpless. That was the only service available on this route. The bus stopped every few minutes to pick up and drop off passengers. Dad objected a couple of times but was ignored. When we reached Satkhira it was late afternoon. Chachu were informed about our arrival. He and Minu Apa were waiting for us in the bus stand. Dad climbed down the bus and hugged Chachu, his eyes welling up. It was not very apparent under normal conditions how deeply he felt about his older brother.

"How are you, bhaijan?"

"We are fine. We are okay. Never thought we'll see you guys again. What a war it was!" Chachu couldn't hold his tears as he replied.

Minu apa observed me with a surprised look." You grew up quite a bit!"

"Do you expect me to be little always?" I trivially said.

Minu apa hit me on the back affectionately. "You are not that big yet, big guy! Who is this little boy? Where did you find him?"

Milky giggled as she diverted her attention toward him. Soon Minu apa completely forgot about my presence and started to cuddle with little Milky. I felt a little jealous. Looked like all the love and attention I used to get before had to be shared with Milky now. Growing up wasn't as trouble free as it seemed. Anyway, when dad told me, "Khoka make sure that all the stuff are loaded in the rickshaws" I had a different type of feelings. I wasn't a kid anymore and was now a dependable person. It felt pretty good.

There was an even bigger crowd waiting to greet us in Chachu's house. The whole neighbourhood had gathered there. It was a common knowledge that we were confined in West Pakistan during the war and two years after the independence. They all were very curious to know about our lives. The questions came in incessantly. Where we lived? What we ate? Did they put us in jail? Finally when everybody returned home we all sighed in relief. My parents were aiming to leave for the village the next day. There was no need to carry everything with us. Hence they needed a little time to repack some essentials for the trip. We chatted very late into the night. We were to start around noon next day. Minu apa was coming with us too. Kaliganj was only about twenty miles from Satkhira. In a bus it could take more than couple of hours. Dad decided to travel in a scooter. I could barely sleep in excitement.

Next morning it started to rain lightly. Rain was pretty common in Bangladesh. It was part of life. It didn't stop anybody from travelling. Nobody seemed worried. But everybody agreed it was a nuisance. Six of us were planning to ride in one scooter, a vehicle built to carry only four. Which meant some of us would have to get more or less wet on the way. We had no other choice. Chachi pressed us to eat our lunch before starting. We quickly ate and climbed into the scooter that Chachu had fetched walking to the scooter stand with his umbrella. Mom sat at the back seat with Minu apa, Rushi and Milky. Dad and I squeezed into the driver's seat flanking him on both sides. This was a common practice and the scooter drivers did not object.

Sitting comfortably in mom's lap Milky curiously looked around and drivelled cheerfully. Where were we going? Why? What was a grandpa? Was there any cows? Could he ride a cow? We had to chuckle at the rate and manner of his questions. The rain stopped but the road was wet forcing automobiles to go slowly. Not ours though. The driver shot through the road overtaking whoever came ahead, totally disregarding the road conditions. It was a narrow one lane road, overtaking meant moving into the lane with oncoming traffic. The roads were busy and overtaking seemed like a risky business. Several times we narrowly made it back to our lane. However, the driver didn't seem to be concerned at all. This was probably part of his regular chore driving on these roads. We were away for a while and were not at all comfortable. Mom warned the driver on regular interval. "Son, drive carefully. There's no need to rush."

There was a bus coming at us, overlapping on both lanes. This was enough to terrify us; however, our driver didn't seem to care much as he smiled patiently to mom's warning and moved to the shoulder to create enough room to pass safely. Something seriously went wrong at this point. It happened quickly, almost in a blink, like an absurd dream. The bus bumped into us, forcing the small scooter into rolling on its side and thrown into the paddy field next to the road. I tried to move but couldn't. My leg was stuck somewhere. I saw dad jerking himself out from under the scooter. There was lot of blood on him. He had cuts but the location was not clear. The driver had serious head injuries. He looked weak, lethargic. His wound could be deadly. I looked back to check on mom. She had numerous cuts on her forehead with blood spraying out. She must have had sensed the accident was going to happen because she sheltered Milky with her body wrapped around him. Milky was unhurt but was howling at the top of his voice. Minu apa looked unhurt. I saw blood on Rushi's forehead suggesting she probably had a cut. Panicked, Rushi jumped out of the scooter and ran into the paddy fields, crying. Dad called her out several times but she didn't seem to hear and continued to run away.

A few farm hands were working in the fields nearby who had seen the accident and came to help us. They brought back Rushi from the paddy fields. Rushi looked possessed and kept on kicking and screaming making it difficult for the poor farmer who was holding her in his lap. The bus that hit us continued to charge ahead. However, to our relief, soon it slowed down to a total stop a few hundred yards away from the accident spot. We later found out that the passengers of the bus had forced the driver to stop.

Several of the passengers came running at us to offer their help. If it wasn't for them we wouldn't be able to get to the hospital quickly and get necessary treatment. A few men pushed the scooter on its wheels. I was still stuck inside. My left leg was caught under the gear. I could not pull it out as I had no strength or feelings there, not even pain. As two-three men pulled on the gear it loosened a little, enough for dad and a volunteer to quickly free me. I tried to stand on my legs but couldn't and fell helplessly on the ground. I could not put any weight on my left leg. Dad picked me up in his lap and carried me into the bus that had now backed up near us.

As we all boarded the bus the floor turned red with the blood that streamed out of the injuries. Looking at mom my heart sunk. Her face was covered in thickened red blood and sprinkled white material, possibly tissues from her cuts. I wasn't sure about my injuries yet but as there was no pain I felt pretty normal. We were driven directly to the Satkhira Central Hospital. After initial checkups we got the full damage report. Mom had two cuts on her forehead; each required four-five stitches. None of them were serious! Thanks God! Rushi needed three-four stitches as well. Dad's cut was on his thigh. It was deep but fortunately missed the vein. As for me, my upper left leg bone was broken into two pieces.

The same evening I returned to Chacha's house with my leg plastered in thick white mold. A separate bed was set for me in a conveniently located room on the first floor. The plastered leg went up on a sling attached to the frame of the bed and stayed there full time. I had never felt so miserable in my whole life. The most painful was the itching inside the plaster. Sometimes I felt like going crazy with multiple spots begging for a scratch, places where even the ruler wouldn't reach. Who knew such misery was waiting for me on my return to Bangladesh? I wept in despair days after days.

However, not everything was bad. Soon I started to see some good sides of it too. Everybody in the household took turns to take care of me - feeding me, cleaning me and giving me company. Relatives and family acquaintances travelled from far to see me. Dad, mom and Rushi healed up quickly. If my leg didn't break we could have made the trip to the village home. They didn't want to go without me. As a result folks from village came to see me. Dadu, dadi and Jhima came first. Shocked to see me lying on my back with my plastered leg hanging from a sling jhima broke into tears. "Oh my God! What you guys have done to my Khoka?"

The few days she stayed she barely moved from my side. Unfortunately they had to leave soon as the labourers were working back in the farm house and they needed to be present. I was hoping Rani apa would come soon but news came that they won't be able to come now. Mama was very busy at school. Final exams were approaching fast. He had many duties to perform. They were planning to come after the exams. Nana also sent news that he would come as soon as possible. Both mentioned that whoever came first would bring Rani apa with him. I sighed. I wasn't going anywhere. Doctors said it could take me a few months to heal.

In the meantime talk of us going back to Dhaka came up. There was little chance of me getting proper treatment in such small town hospital. I felt disappointed. The hope of seeing Rani apa this time around shrunk considerably.

After about three weeks I was taken back to the hospital for another check up. An x-ray revealed that the bones were not placed properly and if left alone could join slightly overlapping. That meant I might end up having to hobble all my life. A decision was taken to cut down the plaster and try to set the bones in right place. Next day I was carried to the hospital again. The nightmare that took place after that was something that I could never describe. Five – six adult men held my broken leg from two ends and started to pull in the opposite direction. The pain was so excruciating that I screamed and moaned vehemently trying to get away from the stronghold. Dad had grabbed my torso tightly to the bed. "A little longer, dear; just a little longer." He continuously pleaded. The pulling went for about five minutes. It felt like eternity. Finally when it stopped I wept in joy. A new plaster was put on. The doctors didn't look happy. They were doubtful if the approach worked. Dad decided to return to Dhaka as soon as my new plaster dried up. This took four - five days.

The day before we started for Dhaka nana, mama and Rani apa showed up in Satkhira. Rani apa looked sad at my immobile, helpless condition. Every time we got together we ran around, climbed trees, swam in the ponds – all the kiddie things. This was an unusual situation for us. She had grown up a little bit, the childish restlessness seemed to be gone, re-placed by a slight matured demeanour, though not like an adult.   She brought me some tamarind seed biscuits from Uncle Jobbar's store. I ate them with great satisfaction. Milky seemed to like them too and returned for more. Later it turned out he was more interested in feeding the chickens chachi kept.

Rani apa mentioned since the liberation the overall situation in the villages had turned even worse. Mama was seriously pondering about moving to Khulna. He was looking for a job there. If things worked out then he would definitely make the move. He would have to employ somebody to take care of his farmland back in the village, but that was a minor obstacle. I voiced my total approval in anticipation that I could see her whenever we visited Khulna.

Dad rented a microbus to take us to Dhaka. With my leg on plaster I couldn't have travelled in a bus. We started pretty early next morning. Mom held nana and cried for long time. For the first time in my life I understood why she cried. Under her tough, often bi-polar personality there was a help-less, emotional little girl who never fully grew up. Rani apa held my hand. "You'll be alright." She said. "We'll pick mangoes again. When you can walk come back. Won't you?"

I nodded. I would. The corners of my eyes be-came wet for no apparent reason. I had travelled this far for nothing. I couldn't even make it to the villages. I could clearly hear the call of the beautiful greener-ies and the far stretched fields. Once back to Dhaka dad would return to work, I'll eventually have to go to school, once my leg cured. Who knew when would we be able to come back again?

Rani apa and many others walked behind our microbus as it slowly advanced over the gravel road heading to the main street. I watched them as long as I could see. Deep inside my throat a knot formed, I couldn't even swallow. Perhaps I was just as emo-tional as mom was.

Chapter 17

As soon as dad returned to work he was posted in Jessore. He felt he couldn't go there leaving me in that condition. He applied for reconsideration explaining my situation. He was reassigned to Dhaka Cantonment. We all sighed in relief. Dad rented an apartment in Mirpur 1. There were several multi storied apartment buildings there. We moved to the building numbered 'E', on the fourth floor. There was no chance of us getting a suitable housing in the army quarters. We tried to get settled in our new apartment.

A lot of families lived in these buildings. Most apartments were quite small. Ours was a one bed-room unit. We placed a bed in the living room and converted it into a second bedroom. The one good thing was that every renter also received a small piece of land for gardening behind the building. Mom didn't waste any time. She prepared the soil and quickly planted varieties of vegetables. In my absence Rushi gave her a hand. Lying down on my bed I got progress report from her on daily basis. There were kids in plentiful, which was something that both Rushi and Milky really appreciated. There was a girl about the same age as Rushi lived right next door. Soon two of them became best friends. The

good part about it was that Rushi's crying and nagging reduced to a comfortable level.

The broken bones in my leg were on the way
to heal. After coming back to Dhaka the plaster was
reopened. Some additional tests were conducted
and my unfortunate leg was wrapped up in plaster
again. The highly qualified doctors who examined me
opined that even though the bones were not fully
aligned and would probably attach to each other
slightly overlapping, it wouldn't have much impact in
the long run considering my young age. Over time I
would be able to use the leg in a way as if nothing
had ever happened. Dad's primary concern was
whether one of my legs became shorter than the
other. He was told such concern was unfounded. We
all hoped for the best, especially me. Would I be able
to play soccer with a leg shorter than the other?

Lying on my back I anxiously counted days.
Dad bought me some books to help me pass time.
Slowly I started to get consumed into them. The
translated children's books from Russian literature
amazed me. Receiving the book 'Malachite's basket'
as a gift I could barely stop my tears. I didn't know
how many times I had read that book. Very soon I
drifted from the reality of the world and started to
fall in love with the magical realm of stories. Beside
my bed books piled up like dwarf mountains. Finally
three months passed and the happiest day of my life
arrived. The plaster was cut off my leg. Doctors examined my leg and confirmed that everything was

fine. First few days I couldn't walk at all. I was even afraid to put any pressure on that foot. It didn't even feel like my own leg. Slowly the fear disappeared. In couple of weeks I was running.

Surprisingly, I found out that even though crowded, living in a colony wasn't so much of a bad thing after all. Within days I made dozens of friends. In the open fields of Mirpur we roamed around in bunches, played soccer for hours, visited the nearby zoo or ventured to the river, a tributary of Buriganga, which flowed not too far from our colony. Suddenly life presented me with all the gifts that I had always asked for. Who ever imagined that here in the big city of Dhaka I would get such portal to nature? I slipped out of the apartment escaping mom's watchful eyes at every opportunity I got. Finding a company was never an issue in the colony. We ventured in new directions every day. No matter how much mom scolded or pleaded it never was enough to stop me. My boyhood and Milky's childhood together built a wonderful mixture. He loved me very much and followed me like a shadow. I didn't want to go anywhere without him either.

Dad admitted us in a private school located in Mirpur 2. I was in grade four, Rushi two, Milky in the play group. An employee of the school walked us to the school and brought us back after school. I made some more friends, boys and girls, played tags during the recess in the playground. After returning from school I rushed through the homework and waited eagerly for the late afternoon when all the boys would come out to the field. As soon somebody called my name I jumped up, slipped into my shoes and ran out of the home. Milky knew things would happen too quickly so he usually had his shoes on. Before mom even had a chance to stop us we would be way out of her reach. There were vast fields on the other side of the narrow uphill road that went into the zoo. That was where we, fifteen- twenty boys, played soccer until it was too dark to identify the ball any longer. We roared, screamed, yelled, sometimes even fought, but above all had the fun of our lives. Upon returning home mom would grab me by the ears.

"Didn't you hear I was calling out for you?" My distress was Rushi's pleasure. She would giggle cheerfully.

Very soon we had a bigger change in our lives. Dad didn't like to work in the army any more. First of all, many of his junior officers were either senior to him or ranked same as him. Secondly the freedom was limited. There was no telling when he would get posted where. There was some agitation during Captain Sujon's trial. Captain Sujon and some of his friends tried to scare the witnesses off. Dad wasn't a person to get intimidated so easily. He did become a witness. However, at the end somehow the case got settled. All together, dad lost his interest to serve the army any more. The problem was getting out with honour. He joined in 1970. Normally he wouldn't be able to retire before 1980. Fortunately in mid 1974 Bangladesh government provided an opportunity to voluntarily retire from army. Dad took it.

After retiring from army he started to work as a medical general practitioner. He was practically unknown as a physician in the area. The economic situation in the country was not very good either. People didn't have much to go on. Dad sat in a pharmacy mornings and evenings as a resident doctor. He got few patients. We started to have difficulties in meeting the ends. I had to beg mom just for ten cents to buy a tamarind treat. However, that didn't stop us from anything. Good hearted vendors gave us treats in advance. At an opportune time I moved a quarter from dad's money bag and paid them off. The feeling of guilt was there but wasn't strong enough to sacrifice the delicious sweet and sour treats and the milk ice creams. I couldn't just buy for myself! I also had to get something for Rushi and Milky if they asked which they always did. Being an older brother wasn't an easy thing.

Life went on. We lived through bad and good times, made friends, played cheerfully in the open fields and slowly but surely became another small stream in the collection of millions of streams that combined made our beautiful and independent country. Along with innumerable kids we three siblings continued to grow and eventually became part of the larger existence.

The End

www.ingramcontent.com/pod-product-compliance
Lightning Source LLC
Chambersburg PA
CBHW070818120626

46556CB00002B/566